Gaining Hope
Claiming Charity
Having Prudence

Lottery Brides
Saving Sarah
Discovering Daisy

Blood Magic Volume One
Warrior's Dawn
Shifter's Delight

Finding Home

Anthology
Brit Party: Maggie's Ménage

BLOOD MAGIC
Volume One

Warrior's Dawn

Shifter's Delight

LACEY THORN

Blood Magic Volume One
ISBN # 978-0-85715-394-4

Interior text design by Claire Siemaszkiewicz
Total-E-Bound Publishing

Published in 2010 by Total-E-Bound Publishing, Think Tank, Ruston Way, Lincoln, LN6 7FL, United Kingdom.

Total-E-Bound Publishing is an imprint of Total-E-Ntwined Limited.

Manufactured in the USA.

Barbara,
Happy Reading!
Lacey Thorn

WARRIOR'S DAWN

Dedication

To the staff at Total-E-Bound publishing, no book would be possible without all of your hard work. And to Claire, who takes the time and effort to make every book that much better! You guys are the best!

Prologue

She was in love. In fact she would always love Mikkel, her husband. Not even death had stopped it and soon, very soon, she would be with her love once more.

Queen Ona took another glance at her sleeping twins Aslan and Aurora. It mattered little how they were sired or who raised them. It only mattered that they were hers, a link to the throne that she would never see again after this night. All she could do now was prepare the way for both of her children as best she could.

Aslan would be okay. His birth father would see to that. Her son would one day grow to be King. He had enough of her in him to be a great leader for their people. She bent low peering into his cradle. He was a beautiful boy and she had little doubt he would grow to be a handsome man. She placed her lips to his forehead and just held still for a moment. Then with a sigh she placed her forehead to his and with deep concentration she planted her memory inside her son's mind.

"When the time is right, my love, you will remember. My knowledge shall be yours." She glanced into his beautiful baby blue eyes praying that her brother would return soon to guard her son. "May you always feel my love as a warmth that surrounds you. May you see my smile in the stars and know that you are blessed."

Blinking away the tears that were already forming in her eyes she turned to where his twin sister Aurora lay. Her daughter would not be so protected. Her daughter would be a warrior like her mother and that would be her kiss of death if Ona left her here. The man who sought her death would also see that Aurora never lived to claim her right as defender. The king ruled the kingdom. But it was the queen that ruled the sword, and the sword that truly ruled the people. He wanted to change that, wanted to change the way the king and queen were decided, but it was bound by the blood of the goddess they prayed to and thus unbreakable.

The title of queen was a birthright and would not be bestowed on the woman her son would marry. It would go to her daughter, her blood. She looked at Aurora, named for Ona's mother and she took a shaky breath as a sob wanted to tear loose. She would never see her grow, never be there for all of a woman's firsts that her daughter would experience. But she would see that Aurora lived to have all of those firsts. With her last breath she would ensure that Aurora lived.

She looked deep into her daughter's blue gaze and smiled. "You'll begin the salvation of us all. Your blood shall start what his shall finish. When the time is right, you shall draw the sword and become the strength as is your birthright. You'll grow strong and smart. You'll laugh. And you'll love. You'll lose and you'll find. My heart breaks for all you will face. But rest assured that you will not stand alone. Time will bring you all together. And a common enemy shall bind you tight." She bent low to place a kiss on her daughter's brow. "You are my daughter. Know my strength, know my love, and call upon them as you need."

"Please don't go," Lydia begged as she walked into the room.

"I have no choice," Ona told her friend. Lydia would keep Ona's secret just as Ona had always kept hers.

"He will kill you," Lydia stated.

"Yes," Ona agreed. "He will."

"Then don't do this," Lydia cried. "We need you."

"If I do not go, he will kill us all," Ona replied her gaze going back to her children.

"We will fight for you," Lydia declared.

"It is my choice," Ona said softly. "And I choose to do what is best for everyone. The death of one to save the many."

"How can your death be good for anyone?" Lydia cried.

"You will see," Ona said. "But first I must ask something of you."

"Anything," Lydia promised. "I will do anything."

"I was hoping you would say that," Ona smiled. "I ask the most important task of you. Take my daughter and flee back to your people. He must not find her until the time is right."

Lydia held her sobs back admirably as she nodded and Ona was touched by the love her friend felt for her. "And Lydia," Ona reached out to place her hand on Lydia's still flat tummy. "He must not know of the child you carry. All of your lives depend on it."

Lydia gasped and Ona knew that Lydia wondered how she knew about the recently conceived child. But Ona knew all. She knew Serena's soon to be born daughter had to be protected as well. That was why she had the priestess take the sword and hide it before making her promise to flee to the temple of the goddess. She knew of the woman he kept prisoner, of the things he did to her, and of the child only just beginning to form into life inside her. She knew she must die and in the aftermath of her death the other three women must make their escapes. Two of the escapes were already set in motion. She would see to the last when she began her walk of death.

This was vitally important to the vision that Ona had been given. It was clear to her that the children must be saved and that was only possible if the mothers were. Her vision had shown her that when the time was right their children would meet and together they would conquer an evil more powerful than Ona had ever seen. What that evil was hadn't been shown nor how the children would find each other. She only knew that it would start with her daughter Aurora and end with her son Aslan.

Holding that vision close she turned back to her friend and told Lydia what she needed her to do, what she must do.

"When you hear the commotion you must take up Aurora and flee," Ona told Lydia. "They will head here first. His guard. They must only find Aslan. They will guard my son with their lives. But you must be gone before they get here."

Lydia nodded her agreement and Ona reached out to take her friend into a fierce hug. "Sister of my heart, know that what you do for me is the greatest gift of all. Guard her and raise her as a sister to your child. They will need the bond to conquer the battles that lie ahead."

She could see the questions in Lydia's eyes, could see her struggling to hold them back and knew that she had chosen the right woman to protect and rear her daughter.

"Tell her of me. The woman you knew, not the queen. Tell her of my love, of my joy at her birth. Tell her she has my eyes, my heart, and when the time is right she will know the power of her birth. Prepare her, train her, but do not raise her to be queen. That is a journey she must begin on her own. She may know of me but not of this place or anything that lies here. Promise me that."

"I promise," Lydia swore.

Ona took a deep breath and closed her eyes for just a moment. She saw Mikkel, her love and knew his strength and pride in what she was doing. With her death chaos would ensue, saving lives. With her death, *his* fate would be sealed. It saddened her. If only things could have been different. They could have stayed friends. But everything happened for a reason. The goddess gave and took as the hands of fate played. And her fate had led her here, to this walk, to this death.

She slipped the key into her pocket. She had no idea how she would manage this part yet, but she would. The native must be freed. Her journey would be the hardest, the longest, and the most painful. But the woman was a descendent of the land itself, and she carried a strength unknown to others. Her child would grant her justice.

Together they would all form a new throne, a new kingdom, a new power. Ona smiled. She played but a small part in what they would accomplish. But every small part was important. With one last glance to her children she slipped from the room and began the walk to her death.

"I'm coming my love," she said and only those who didn't know her assumed she spoke of the man she was on her way to see.

Chapter One

Aurora watched as the group of natives left the camp her people called home. Not for the first time she wished she could go with them. She wanted to see more of this land and she knew that they would be the ones to travel with. What little she had seen of their powers was amazing. Rory stopped in front of her and Aurora smiled at the beautiful girl. Her cocoa brown skin was flawless and the perfect backdrop for her lush golden brown curls. But it was the green amber cat's eyes that had her continuing to look at Rory.

"I'll miss you my friend," Rory said and held her arm out to Aurora.

Aurora took it, grasping her fingers around Rory's forearm just above her elbow as Rory did the same. "Safe travels Rory."

"Something hovers in the air," Rory said. "It is dark and tinged with the touch of evil. I hear your name on the wind."

"I'm evil?" Aurora questioned trying to lighten the mood but Rory didn't crack a smile.

"Just watch and be safe," Rory told her squeezing her hand on Aurora's forearm before releasing her. "Something comes for you."

Aurora smiled, more than used to Rory's omens. "I will watch, my friend. I promise."

But the graveness didn't leave Rory's eyes. Finally she nodded and walked back to her people, was swallowed into the middle of them then almost as if a veil had fallen, the entire group disappeared. It was always that way and Aurora still had no idea how they did it.

"Aurora," Lydia called and she hurried over to where the woman who had raised her stood with her birth daughter Lynx.

"Yes, Mama," she said and she saw the brief flash of sorrow in Lydia's eyes before the woman smiled. It was always that way when Aurora called her Mama. And she knew that Lydia thought of Aurora's birth mother and not for the first time Aurora wondered what she wasn't being told about that woman.

"Lynx said she heard Rory tell you something," Lydia stated and Aurora sent a glare to her baby sister.

"Little sisters should keep their mouths shut," she said.

Lynx just laughed and stretched making her already long lean body even more so. "But then I'm not really the little one."

And Aurora couldn't help it. She laughed. Lynx was indeed the taller of the two. She had the lines of her people. She stood five-foot-ten with a lean body corded with the muscles of a shifter. Aurora wasn't that much shorter standing at five-foot-eight but she had thicker muscles, muscles that bunched and bulged. She was strong and she loved it.

There had been a time when she cried because she couldn't shift like her sister and mother, like most of the people where they lived. She wanted to be a cat or a wolf or whatever animal she was given as protector. But that wasn't her fate in life. Hers lay elsewhere. And it wasn't until she picked up her first weapon that she found her calling. She couldn't shift but what she could do was wield any weapon at hand with an inner knowledge that had her expert at them all. But for some reason she favoured the sword, the feel of the metal in her hand was like coming home.

"Size is irrelevant, baby sister," she said instead and Lynx just gave that precocious grin of hers.

"Aurora," Lydia said and Aurora sighed at the worry in her eyes.

"I'll be careful, Mama, I promise." And she would. She always was. But she had plans for later tonight that she wouldn't change. Tonight was the night she finally let Domi and Nado catch her. Tonight was the night she made them hers.

"I'm not sure that I like that look in your eyes," Lydia sighed and made Aurora grin. Lydia wouldn't like it if she knew. Lydia had always discouraged Domi and Nado from pursuing Aurora. She told Aurora that she was too young to mate but Aurora knew that there was more to it than that. For some reason Lydia didn't want her to make a more permanent tie here. Once she had worried that it was because Lydia didn't really love her. But she knew better now. There was a reason but Aurora just hadn't quite figured it out yet.

"Don't worry," Aurora assured Lydia. "I will be safe." And she would. Domi and Nado would guard her with their lives. Tonight she would enter a new phase of her life. That of mate. And even here she would be different.

For she wouldn't choose between the two men who were more like brothers than friends. She would mate with them both and defy anyone to say a word against it, or any woman to try and break it. Tonight she would stake her claim and tomorrow all would know of it.

Domi watched Aurora from his place in the tree line. He was in his panther form, his guardian spirit, and his senses were high. He could hear the words spoken and gave a growl at the look of worry on Lydia's face. She would try to stop them yet again if she knew what he and Nado had in store for tonight. But there would be no more hiding, no more sneaking a kiss here or there. Tonight they would make Aurora theirs and in the morning they would no longer hide.

With a growl he sprang from the tree and headed into the woods to hunt. He would provide a bounty of fresh cooked game for his mate. She would never fear that he and Nado couldn't provide for all her needs.

Nado watched Domi leap and still he stood. He had yet to take his cat form instead choosing to blend back into the surrounding fauna in his human form. He had always been a little jealous of the fact that Domi kept the ebony skin of their panther form even when in his human skin while Nado went back to the paler flesh of their ancestors. Domi looked more like a native than a shifter. But he was all panther. And though some might question none who truly knew him ever would.

Tonight they would make Aurora theirs. He could feel his cock growing hard at the thought of her pale skin between him and Domi. She always looked like a golden goddess next to Domi's dark form with her curtain of blonde curls hanging past her shoulders and the big blue orbs of her eyes. She was truly the most beautiful woman he had ever seen and he could barely wait to officially make her his, theirs. They would all be crossing lines tonight.

Though many of the other tribes formed triads, the shifters didn't. They formed pairs. But from tonight on, it would be the three of them, always and forever. He let a smile form on his lips and joy fill his heart. Tonight they would be as one. He wanted it to be the most perfect night of Aurora's life.

He turned and with a leap shifted in midair to his panther. He took off after Domi, easily tracking the man who had always been like a brother to him. This time tomorrow they would no longer be a duo but a trio. The night couldn't fall fast enough to please him.

Aurora checked once more to make sure that Lynx was really asleep before creeping as quietly as she could from their room. She could not afford to let anyone catch her. There was no stopping what was meant to be, and she, Domi and Nado were meant. She couldn't contain the big grin that spread across her face, didn't even try to. She wanted this perhaps even more than they did.

Finally in the open air she took a deep breath and almost screamed when a hand wrapped around her waist and pulled her back against a long hard body. It was the other hand that popped over her mouth that stopped her. Her muscles tensed as she prepared to fight. Until the smooth voice of Domi sounded in her ear.

"Going to fight me, love?" he whispered.

Her whole body relaxed into his embrace. "Domi you almost got your ass kicked."

His low chuckle washed over her. "Hmmm... Sounds like a mood setter to me." And he pressed closer so that she could feel the ridge of his rock-hard cock against her back. She moaned and leant back into him. And that quickly she had him grabbing her hand and pulling her towards the woods and the cabin that awaited them.

Her grin was back in place. Maybe Domi and Nado were as excited as she was. Hell, he had her practically running to get to the cabin. But then this would be the first night of their lives together as mates. From this point on they would no longer sleep alone. They would share a home now. The one that Domi and Nado had already built for them.

Domi stopped just outside the door and turned to face her. He was so beautiful to her. She loved the way that he kept the dark ebony skin of his panther. Loved the tight black curls on his head and the deep black of his eyes. He was full of shadow and light all at once. At six feet he wasn't that much taller than her and they fit so well together. She leaned into him and hugged him tightly. He caressed her face and tilted it up so that she could see him.

"Are you sure this is what you want?" he asked softly.

"Have you changed your mind?" she asked instead.

"Never," he declared.

"And neither have I," she promised.

"I only ask because there will be no going back after this night," he told her. "There will be no you, no me, no Nado. We will be as one. No longer will we face our battles alone, but together."

"I know all that Domi," she assured him. "Are you and Nado sure that you want to be with me? No matter what road lies ahead for me?"

"Wherever it leads you, we will follow," he told her and bent to brush his lips across hers. It was meant to be a small token she was sure but they both needed more.

She didn't know who changed it, but soon they were devouring each other, their tongues fighting for control of the kiss. His hand found her breast under the loose shirt she wore and his long fingers plucked and pinched her already pebbled nipple. She groaned and rubbed wantonly against him, somehow managing to wedge one of his muscular thighs between her legs. Only their leathers separated them and it felt so good to grind her flesh along his muscle.

But before things could go any further the door opened behind them and the vision of Nado caught and held her gaze. The man was truly beautiful. His skin had the golden glow of the sun and his shoulder length brown waves were kissed by it as well. But it was his eyes that she could drown in. Such a light shade of brown with flecks of yellow in them. Domi might keep his panther skin but Nado kept his cat's eyes.

"Starting without me?" he queried as he stood there, a smile on his lips.

"Just warming her up," "Domi grunted as he reluctantly pulled his hand from her shirt.

"She looks pretty warm to me," Nado laughed.

Aurora grinned. "Burning hot," she swore.

"Then we should definitely do something to cool you down," Nado said and moved out of the doorway so that they could all move inside.

The room was laid out beautifully and she wondered how long they had worked on it. The table was filled with food. Cheese and fruit, bread, and what she was sure was fresh game, caught and prepared just for her. Wine was there as well and she desperately wanted a drink to wet her suddenly dry throat. A fire blazed and before it several blankets had been laid out. She knew what was planned and although she wanted it desperately she was still a little nervous.

She had never been with a man before, never cared to. It was different with Domi and Nado. They called to her soul. As much as she had run from them at first there was just no getting away. And she was glad that they had continued to pursue her even after Lydia had warned them away. She loved them. That simple and that complex. She loved them both and didn't want to be without them.

"It's all so beautiful," she said as she entered and shut the door behind her. "You went to so much trouble."

"There is no trouble when it comes to you," Nado said.

"Except that which you cause," Domi added and she laughed as Nado glared at him. Nado would want the seduction to be smooth and all about complimenting her. But Domi's nature wouldn't allow that. Such opposites at times and yet so alike in many ways, Domi and Nado were quite simply perfect for her.

"And if I promise not to cause any tonight?" she asked unable to mask her grin.

"We can only hope for the best," Domi said and even Nado had to laugh.

"What would you like first?" Nado asked. "Food? Wine?"

She stepped into him, ran her hands up his chest to his shoulders. He was slightly taller than her and Domi standing at six-foot-one. She let her hands glide over his shoulders to tangle in his hair. She loved his hair almost as much as he seemed to love hers. She used its length to tug his face down to hers. Her lips skimmed up his throat so that she could nibble along his jaw before making her way to his ear and the licking the lobe there before nipping it with her teeth.

"How about you?" she breathed into his ear and the last bit of nerves were gone. "How about we eat later?"

Domi moved up behind her cocooning her between their bodies. "Or we could just start with dessert," he whispered in her ear before licking and sucking at the lobe.

"Yes," she moaned. "I've waited too long for this, for you, both of you. I don't want to wait any longer."

"Then you won't," Nado said and in what seemed like a blink of her eyes she found herself lying down on the covers in front of the fire watching two gorgeous men undress for her eyes alone.

Not much to watch as they only wore leather pants and soft boots. Neither man ever wore a shirt and she liked that about them, liked to watch the muscles of their chests and abdomens ripple in the sunlight. They were beautiful, and soon hers and hers alone.

Domi was the first to shove his pants down past his cock and her mouth watered at the sight of it. It jutted from his body thick and heavy already glistening with a drop of cum on its tip. Without thought she moved to her knees and while his hands were busy with his pants she explored it with her mouth. He gasped and she felt his entire body tighten up. But she wanted his taste, loved the way it exploded on her tongue as she ran it around the flushed head before sucking it into her mouth. He tasted like the game they hunted, salty and wild and she groaned at the pleasure of finally having him in her mouth.

Her hands went up to clench his bare hips and his brushed through her hair. She felt the tension in his body and yet his touch was soft. She could feel his pants tangled around his knees and moved her hands lower to help him. Slowly she tugged them down leaning away from him with her body while keeping her mouth working the head of his cock. Finally she moved away, letting him slide reluctantly from her lips so that she could pull his shoes off and slide his pants all the way free.

But when she would have moved back he stopped her. "More of that and I won't be able to function at all. And I want our first time together for me to be deep inside your pussy."

She blushed. She just couldn't help it. She wanted the same thing but she was hungry for more as well. She saw movement beside her and turned to see Nado just finishing shedding his clothes. His cock was longer than Domi's, not as thick, but it had a wicked curve to it that she wanted to feel. She almost pounced on him and he laughed until the moment her lips wrapped around him and she sucked him in.

His taste was just the opposite of Domi. More subtle and so sweet, like the berries that grew on the vine. He didn't stretch her mouth as wide but she couldn't fit as much of his length in. She ran her tongue over and around what she could and let her fingers work the sac that hung beneath, enjoying the way it grew taunt and drew up closer to his body. The male anatomy was so interesting and so enjoyable. She could spend hours learning them both, laving and exploring them. But Nado could take no more than Domi had.

He tugged her away from him then groaned as she stuck her tongue out to continue caressing him even after he'd popped free of her mouth.

"You taste so good," she groaned.

"And soon you may have as much of it as you want, whenever you want," he promised her. "But for now I want to taste you. We both want to finally see you naked and taste the exotic flavours of your skin."

"Yes," she breathed and let them pull her to her feet once more.

"Then let's get you out of all these clothes," Nado said as he reached for her loose shirt, the only article of clothing that she wore that differed from them. Domi knelt before her and worked the laces on her leathers free. He tugged them down exposing the pink slit of her cunt and paused to lean in. Instead of tasting her as she thought he would he only closed his eyes and breathed deeply. But the pleasure that lit his eyes when he opened them back up made her shake with desire.

Finally she was naked. Domi tugged her down beside him and leaned her back onto the blankets. Nado knelt at her other side. The fire was warm, the blankets were soft, and she was more than ready for what came next. She undulated and watched their eyes flare. With a groan both men reached for her and she knew the time of waiting had finally come to an end.

Chapter Two

Domi reached for Aurora's breasts palming and squeezing the globes in his hands before moving out to the nipples, pinching and tugging at them. She groaned and looked at him. She wanted his mouth on them, on her. Instead he leaned down to kiss her and that was even better. He took possession of her mouth and made her even hungrier for his touch.

She felt hands on her thighs and knew that Nado was there even before he moved between them. His shoulders were wide and he used them to help keep her spread before him. She could only imagine what she must look like. She knew she was already wet with hunger, could feel her juices on her inner thighs. And when Nado groaned she knew he liked what he saw.

"So beautiful, Domi. You should see how pink and wet her cunt is for us," Nado stated as he ran a finger down through her slit coating the digit with her juices.

"She smells sweet," Domi agreed moving back from her mouth to let his gaze move down her body to where Nado held her slit open.

They all watched as Nado brought his wet finger to his mouth and sucked it deep. His eyes closed and he groaned with pleasure. Domi groaned with him.

"Taste?" he asked Nado.

"Divine, like the sweetest nectar you've ever had," Nado said.

Aurora reached down and ran her finger over herself before pushing it briefly inside her pussy and swirling it. Both men stared seeming transfixed by her touching herself. Did they really think that women didn't do that? She snorted as she brought the digit up and held it out to Domi.

"Try for yourself," she told him and with a harsh cry he latched onto her finger and drew it deep into his mouth. He sucked hard working his tongue all over her digit before slowly letting it go.

"Even better knowing you fed it to me," he said and she laughed.

But her laugh was cut short when Nado leaned in and began to lave his tongue over her from pussy to clit. He swirled around the engorged bud of her clitoris and sucked it gently into his mouth. She arched off the covers seeking to get closer to him, to the pleasure. But Domi was there to hold her down. His black eyes were hooded and even darker and she loved the red flush that desire left on his cheeks. He was indeed a beautiful man.

She held his gaze as he moved to her heaving breasts and the tight nipples there. Finally he took one in his mouth and sucked it, working the nipple against the roof of his mouth with his tongue. Then he used his teeth to nip slightly and tug on it. It was good, so fucking unbelievably good that she wanted more. She lifted her arms to his head loving the feel of his short black curls against her palms, loving the sight of his dark flesh against hers.

Nado's tongue was back to tasting her and now his fingers were getting in on the action. Domi used one hand to torture one breast while using his mouth on the other. They were killing her. She was already on fire for them but now she was burning alive. She was arching and moaning and crying out with the bombardment of pleasure. She had one hand on Domi's head and the other on Nado's and went back and forth from tugging them away to pushing them closer. Not that it mattered. They were going to do what they wanted.

"Please," she moaned. "I can't take anymore. Please take me now."

Domi just pulled back and grinned down at her, his hand still wicked on her breast and nipple. Nado pushed a finger deep inside her pussy and began working it in and out of her. Domi just watched and waited. Nado wrapped his lips around her clit and sucked her. One finger became two and she bucked and yelled beneath them. Her body felt tight, like there was a knot in her stomach that was being pulled tighter and tighter. She couldn't take it and shook her head as he continued to work her.

"Relax Aurora," Domi whispered leaning down to her. "Let it come. Stop fighting it."

"I can't," she cried. "Too much. I can't take it."

Domi just smiled and Nado sucked harder, moved his fingers faster in and out then in again. Domi leaned that few inches closer and took her cries into his mouth letting his tongue battle with hers and she could hold back no longer. The knot let loose with a torrent of fire. It shot through her veins spreading in every direction but seeming to centre in her stomach and pussy. She could feel the way she squeezed his fingers, feel the slow pumps he was now giving.

Domi pulled back and grinned at her. She glanced down and found the same look on Nado's face, still glistening with her juices. She lay back, closed her eyes and took a deep breath before slowly releasing it. She was relaxed, more relaxed than she had ever been in her life.

"I like that smile," Domi said and she opened her eyes to see the soft pleasure on his face. Only then did she realise that she was smiling from ear to ear. "That good huh?"

"Ummm…hmmm" she agreed.

"Let's see if I can make it better," he said and moved over her.

At some point Nado had moved from his sprawl between her legs to rest on the blanket beside her. His eyes were closed and he kept licking over his wet lips. She would have laughed but there was just something about knowing that it was her he tasted that was incredibly erotic. She felt Domi's cock brush against her stomach and her eyes went back to him and the way he looked above her.

"You are so beautiful," she said.

Domi laughed, "Shouldn't that be my line?"

"You really are, Domi," she said.

"Then we are a perfect triad," he said

"Yes," she agreed.

"Yes," Nado agreed without opening his eyes.

"Then take me. Unite us completely so that none may try to separate us ever again," Aurora said.

"Never again," he promised and used one hand to seat the head of his cock at her wet pussy. "Ours from this night on."

"Yes," she cried and wrapped her arms around his neck, her legs reaching up to clasp along his hips. "Now, Domi! Fuck me now!"

With a panther's snarl he plunged his cock to the hilt inside her tight pussy and claimed her as his. She was tight, hot and so fucking wet he was afraid he would not be able to control himself long enough to pleasure her again. He took a deep breath and held himself within her, struggling to find that control, but it was not to be. With a cry she lifted against him pressing him just a tad deeper and came. He could feel her flesh squeezing around him and trying to milk his cock.

He fought the animal inside and lost. His cock plunged fast and furious, riding her hard. The human part of him was terrified of hurting her but the way she arched and cried out clinging and clawing at him excited the animal beyond control. So he took and prayed that he gave as well. He heard her screaming and was delighted to realise they were cries of pleasure tearing from her. She enjoyed the animalistic mating, screamed with her pleasure in it. Yes, this was the woman for him, for Nado, a true mate for a panther.

With a roar he came, filling her with him and marking her as his from this moment on. Anyone who came upon her would smell him and know that she was mated. Soon Nado's scent would mark her as well and she would be doubly protected. He glanced down at her and would have been startled to know that it was the golden amber eyes of the panther that looked at Aurora and not those of the man.

"I love you Domi," she said as she continued to experience little orgasms beneath him. "With all I am, I love you."

"Forever, my warrior," he promised. "I will love you forever."

He moved from her and collapsed on his back beside her. She rolled over onto her stomach and put one hand on his chest to rub softly in the hair there. It was as if she needed to touch him and he revelled in that small sign of affection from her. She was his. He glanced over to where Nado still lay on the other side and nodded. It was time for Nado to stake his claim as well.

She felt Nado move on her other side and went to roll onto her back again but his hands caught her hips and stopped her.

"Just come to your knees my love and let me have you like this," Nado said.

She glanced over her shoulder as she came up to her hands and knees and was excited just by the look in his eyes. Her gaze fell to his cock and she groaned. She couldn't wait to feel that wicked curve inside her. And it appeared that Nado couldn't wait either. He didn't use his hands, didn't move them from where they gripped her hips. He just pressed forward and let his cock run through her slit until it slid against her entrance on its own. Then he pressed forward and kept pressing until he was inside her.

She would swear that his cock reached her very womb, he was so long and the wicked curve placed the head high against the wall of her pussy. Every thrust was a hard rub against the nerves there and when he started pounding there was no holding the screams back. It felt so incredible. Where Domi was thick, Nado was long and reached deeper. Each sharp thrust threw her higher towards an immediate orgasm. Her fingers were clenched in the blanket, her head tossing back and forth. The pleasure was so good that she thought she might actually die from it.

"Nado," she screamed his name and was answered by an even quicker, harder pace.

Orgasm ripped through her making her feel like lightening-ravaged earth. Her muscles wouldn't hold her and if not for Nado's grip she would have completely collapsed onto the blanket instead of just her chest falling. He continued thrusting, riding her orgasm and forcing her to as well. She was going to shatter, to just fly into a million pieces. Pleasure like this must be why the shifters only took one mate. She was crazy for taking on two such virile men. Panthers no less.

Nado grunted behind her, lifting her knees from the blanket with his final thrust and she could feel the harsh blast of his essence filling her up. Marked now. That was her last coherent thought. She was marked now, the chosen mate of Domi and Nado. Never again would they be kept apart. A smile bloomed on her lips and even though she didn't open her eyes she felt them there, turning her and stroking over her body with wet cloths.

"Love you," she murmured. "Love you both so much."

"Love you." It was Nado's voice in her ear, his touch on her cheek. "I have loved you since the first."

And she knew what he meant. It had always been her and Nado. She had followed him around like a puppy when they were little and he had never once complained or shifted and ran from her. Eventually when they were teens Domi had joined them, become like a brother to Nado, and they had been together ever since, much to Lydia's displeasure.

Aurora had asked her once why she didn't like Domi and Nado. Lydia has said that it wasn't that she didn't like them. They were good boys. It was just that Aurora was meant for more than their village life. That was fine with Aurora. But she saw no reason why Domi and Nado couldn't go with her.

"Sleep, my warrior," Domi whispered. "Rest while you can," he added with a wicked laugh.

"Yes," she agreed, sleep already tugging at her. "Then we should do all that again to make sure the first time wasn't just beginners' luck."

Both men started laughing and she thought it was a lovely sound to fall asleep to.

She woke several hours later with a mate on either side of her. She stretched and was deliciously sore in all the right places. She sat up slowly and moved quietly so as not to wake them. She just had a quick errand to run and would be back before they even knew she was gone. She slipped into her clothes and shoes, watching them the whole time to make sure she didn't wake them. There was a catch in her heart now because finally they belonged with her. Finally no one would be able to separate them again.

She grinned as she headed out the door closing it softly behind her. She just wanted to talk to Lynx real quick and share the good news with her baby sister. Lynx would be so happy for her. And Lynx would be able to tell Lydia where Aurora was so that their mother wouldn't worry when she couldn't find her. Aurora planned on spending as much time as she could alone with Domi and Nado in the cabin. Then they would all move in together.

She was daydreaming. That was the only reason they caught her unaware. One moment she was happy and the next she was turning to see what had suddenly spooked her. But it was too late. The laser brushed her neck and down she went, falling into a semi-sleep that was anything but restful this time around. She could feel the scrape on her palm, the small bead of blood that was forming there. She wasn't completely out. She wasn't sure why but she played the part anyway, listening for what they might say.

"Are you sure this is the one Wilhelm wanted?" A deep voice but one she had never heard before.

"She's the one he's been looking for all right." Another new voice. Strangers. And they worked for Wilhelm, a name more and more people were becoming familiar with. The man was known for taking what he wanted no matter the cost.

"Remember to be quick and quiet," the first man said. "Aslan is not to know of this."

Aslan. That was the name of the King. Why would Wilhelm want her hidden from Aslan? Why would Wilhelm want her in the first place? Lydia had always said that she was special, that she was meant for a greater purpose but she had never told her what that purpose was. It seemed she would find out soon enough now. And her answers were with Wilhelm.

She was glad that she had mated with Domi and Nado this night. Her mates would follow her no matter where these men took her. Her mates would find her and free her and together they would find out what and who she really was. Finally she would have answers. She just had to be patient and wait for the right time.

She was tossed into the back of a wagon and she barely contained the grunt of pain as she hit against someone else. Someone bigger and not as soft. Someone she thought must be male going from shape and what she could feel. She wasn't going to reach between his legs to be sure though. She had no idea if he was awake or not and she didn't want to find out just yet. One of the men followed her in and grabbed her wrists together in front of her. He tied them with a piece of rope then left her.

She tried to wiggle away but had little success as they started on their journey towards Wilhelm.

"Lie still and reserve your strength," a deep voice said from behind her. "You will need it for what lies ahead."

"Who are you?" she whispered. "What do you know of where they are taking us?"

"I am Micah," he said. "I am Danuja, captured on your shores days ago. I am bound ankles to wrists and have been unable to free myself. I have listened to them speak of you, the lost one that they have spent years searching for."

"The lost one?" she queried. She could feel his hands behind her and guessed that he was tied in front as well which meant these men had no idea what they were doing.

"Their words. You are much sought after by this Wilhelm."

"For what reason?" she asked.

"That I am unsure of," he answered. "I only know that I am to be burned at the stake for having been foolish enough to be captured on this land. Your fate is unknown to me."

Aurora turned so that she could see as much of the man behind her as possible. He was big which was common for his people, most of which were over seven feet tall. His hair was full and thick hanging in braids to his shoulders. But his eyes were golden and they shone brightly from his face.

"When I free myself, I will set you free too," she promised him. "You must be ready to fight with me."

"Yes," he nodded and she wondered if he was earnest or just placating her. "You will find what is meant and all will be well. Don't forget me. Release me and I will guard you with my life."

"Are you a seer?" she asked, remembering vaguely some stories she had heard of his people being able to see certain things.

"No," he laughed. "I was not given such a gift as that one. My gifts are unique though. I can read people. There is a glow around us all that hides nothing. Yours does not show death in your future, and mine disappeared when you were captured and thrown in here with me. You are my salvation and I will protect you with all I am."

She nodded and lay back down quietly in front of him. "When the time is right be ready. It will happen quickly. But I will not forget to set you free. That is my promise Micah."

"I am yours to command," he said and quietly they waited for when the moment would be right.

Chapter Three

"What do you mean she is gone?" Domi thundered at Lynx.

"Who has taken her?" roared Nado.

They had only just dressed after waking to find Aurora gone. It was not hard to figure out where she was and why. She had gone to tell her sister of their mating so that Lydia would not worry. That was how Aurora worked.

Lynx stood her ground and glared at the two men. "Stop shooting daggers at me," she yelled. "This isn't helping us find my sister. She was taken. I heard a noise and found them just in time to see her thrown into a wagon."

"What were you thinking?" Domi yelled again. "You could have been taken with her."

"I was in cat form," she replied. "I chose the small cat for which I am named this time. I was perfectly safe." It was well known that she often had trouble sleeping and roamed the camp at night in cat form. Though it worried some it was accepted by all.

Nado shook his head. Lynx was the only shifter he knew who was not limited to one guardian form. She could take the form of many cats and did. There was magic in her blood that was different even from their own.

"We must go after her," Nado stated the obvious. "Did you see which direction they took her?"

"Yes," Lynx said, "but I took the time to find her mates first since it will be easiest for you to follow what you have marked as your own."

Domi glared but Nado had to laugh. "I assume you won't be staying behind, little sister?" Nado asked though he already knew the answer.

"I can go with you so that you can keep an eye on me," she agreed. "Or I can go on my own. But I am going after my sister. She needs me. I can feel it."

"Then hurry," Domi said as he moved to stuff some things in a bag. "We leave in minutes."

Lynx indicated a bag just outside the door. "Already ahead of you black cat."

Nado grinned again despite the circumstances. He couldn't wait to see the man who would go head to head to tame the wild cat that was Lynx. They would find Aurora soon. And he had little doubt that his warrior would be able to protect herself until they got there. Hell she would probably be waiting on them wondering what had taken them so long.

"Then let's go," Domi interrupted his thoughts as he slung a bag at Nado and headed towards the door.

"Did you leave word for your mother?" Nado asked Lynx not wanting the woman to awaken to both of her daughters missing.

"Yes," Lynx stated.

"Then we go," Nado agreed. He fit the straps of the bag to his chest and shifted knowing it would be snug against him and safe. A shifter didn't need much, but even shifter's could be caught and hurt so they learned to never travel without certain important supplies. A life could depend on it.

At some point Aurora must have slept. She awoke to the sound of voices, laughter and even some yelling.

"What's in the wagon?" It was a voice that rang with authority.

"It is just some supplies for Wilhelm, my king." She recognised the voice from the night before but somehow it was not as confident now.

"You must make your move now," Micah whispered beside her. At some point she had rolled into him—probably seeking warmth—and now lay facing him. "I have freed your hands. Our fate now resides with you."

She took a deep breath and came up to her knees. Her hands must have been free for a while as there was no stiffness or soreness in them. She must be quick and she must get back to free Micah before all was lost. She crept quietly to the back of the wagon and peered out. They were in a tree filled area. There were several horses around and men dressed casually but wearing the brawn of a trained warrior. She could not see the king, nor the men he was speaking with. They must be at the front of the wagon.

She needed a weapon. That was her first order of business. All these men surely would not be here without a weapon on them. But she couldn't find one anywhere. Her eyes scanned everywhere taking in everything she could see. No weapons that she could visibly make out, but she would bet her life they had them.

Frustration was growing when she spied a sword. It was maybe a hundred yards away, an easy enough distance for her to dash across. She couldn't tell if it was in the tree or in the ground just in front of it. It was the most beautiful weapon she had ever seen. The hilt was encrusted with some large jewel that shone brightly. There seemed to be some etching along the part of the blade but at this distance she couldn't be sure what it was. All she knew was that it called to her, like a hum in the blood and demanded she come for it. This was hers to take and it felt as if it had been waiting for her.

Foolish, she knew but she would take what she could get.

"There is a weapon," she whispered to Micah. "About a hundred yards out. I will dash for it. When I pull it I will give a cry the likes of which I'm sure they have never heard. When you hear it, move yourself to the back of the wagon." She glanced back at him. They had used something other than rope to bind him and she could not undo it. She had tried and tried before they finally fell into an exhausted sleep.

"I will free you my friend." It was a promise she meant to keep.

"I will listen for it," he vowed and she prayed to the goddess that he made it with her.

She came up to her toes at the wagon's back opening and took several deep breaths to centre herself. She had but one shot and she intended to make it. Once she leapt from the wagon they would all be after her and her chances would be better if she had the sword in her hand when she faced the men here. One shot. One dash and she would stand and fight.

They were still talking with the king but it was a dull whine in the back of her consciousness now. She was focused, ready. The time was now. With a stealth that would make her mates proud she leapt from the wagon and ran full speed towards the tree and the sword. She heard shouts, heard the clatter of footsteps behind her but she was there, too fast with too much of a lead for them to catch up. There was but one thing to do.

Never slowing her speed she reached down with one hand to grip the hilt of the sword tightly and went up the front of the tree. Doing a back flip she landed on her feet in a crouch one hand to the ground and the other holding the sword aloft. She came up with a cry that rattled the tree tops, but the sight that greeted her was one that shocked her.

Everything had stopped. Every man faced her with a look of wonder on his face and slowly one by one they all dropped to one knee and bowed before her. What the hell was going on? King Aslan stood looking at her from across the distance and as he got closer to her she could see the look on his face. It was one of wonder and love and it confused her greatly.

"You have finally come home," he whispered and reached a hand out to touch her cheek.

She backed away from him still holding the sword in front of her. Even a king could die. "I don't know what you mean. I assure you this journey was not by choice."

"You are Aurora, yes?" he asked just looking at her, and it was easy to see his regal bearing.

"Yes," she answered the truth always better than a lie.

"I don't know where you have been or why," he stated. "I only know that you are returned to us and this is cause for great celebration."

She turned and gave a shake of her head. "You are under the illusion that I meant to be here. That I am staying."

He laughed. "Meant or not by you, here you stand," and he spread his hands wide to indicate where they were. But then his voice lowered and it was as if the next words were meant just for her. "And you must stay."

"Why is that my king?" she queried.

"Because to you I am more than your king," he said and reached his hand back out to her brushing a finger gently over her cheek. "I am your brother."

Shock rolled through her and she honestly didn't know for sure what she would have said. But fate intervened in that moment as she noticed the wagon just start to move. "Stop that wagon," she roared and everyone jumped into action.

Men ran as two panthers burst into the clearing, a small bobcat with them. She knew these cats and suddenly all was well. She ran towards the wagon with everyone else and the cats followed her. Two of King Aslan's men had managed to stop it and when they did the men who worked for Wilhelm took off never once looking behind them. She wanted to kill them and it shocked her as she had never had that desire before. But they stank of evil and she wanted to rid the world of it. She wasn't surprised when the three cats continued following the men.

"Open the back of the wagon," she ordered and wasn't surprised when two men jumped forward to do it.

They all stepped back at the sight of the large man bound there. Aurora went to step forward but it was Aslan that beat her to him. He pulled a dagger from somewhere and with ease cut through the wiry bonds that held Micah.

"Be free my friend," Aslan said.

Micah slowly freed himself from his bonds, rolling his shoulder and stretching his legs out before him to dangle over the back of the wagon. He was even bigger than she thought, easily topping the seven foot mark. He moved to stand and teetered uncertainly for a moment. She went to step forward to help but Aslan stopped her. Micah sent him a nod of thanks.

Men. She thought. *Pride would keep them from a helping hand more often than not.*

Micah came to his feet and slowly made his way a few feet to where she stood. He went down to one knee and bowed his head. "I live to serve you my queen," he said.

"Queen?" she shook her head and glanced at Aslan.

"Your birthright," he answered.

"I'm not doing anything kinky like marrying my brother or anything," she said.

Aslan laughed. "My future wife will not be queen. It is a right of birth that passes through the blood. It goes to keep us close and to give the people a council and not a monarchy. We rule together." He turned to her. "I've missed you like my other half. Have you not felt once that a part of you was missing?"

"Yes," she answered. She'd always felt that something was missing but then why wouldn't she? Raised by a woman other than her mother, in a place where she was not from. She had just accepted how she felt, not knowing the cause, and moved on.

"Twins share a bond even closer than mere siblings," Aslan stated. "I have searched for you since I was old enough to ride."

"I never knew of your existence," she said honestly but her mind was stuck on the *twins* comment. "The woman who raised me did not tell me of you, of this." She gestured around them where the men finally stood watching them.

His face darkened. "You mean the woman who took you when our mother was murdered."

"If she did," Aurora stated with no doubt, "then she did so to save me." She did know that her mother had been murdered. Lydia had told her of that as well as not to believe all that she might hear in relation to that murder.

She reached out for the first time and touched…her brother. "Know this. I had a great childhood. I never once faced a day without love or acceptance. I have a family and I believe I have turned out just fine."

"Your family will be welcome here then," Aslan relented but she could see the anger still within him. There was something there. She would have to find out what. One thing was for sure. She wouldn't be heading back to Lydia and the shifters any time soon.

She saw the men tensing and knew what they were seeing before she turned. Two panthers re-entered the meadow and she had little doubt that they had caught and killed the two men that had kidnapped her. Her mates would have it no other way. Lynx followed them now in the shape of a tiger and she almost laughed with joy knowing that her sister had come for her too. She wondered what Lynx would think of her being a queen.

The two panthers leapt at her and transformed mid-air to land as men on either side of her. Her mates. Her life. They embraced her, each running their hands over all they could of her flesh checking her for injury, reassuring themselves that she was fine. They were so wrapped within one another that they failed to notice the tiger, the man she approached, or the man who approached her.

Lynx stopped in front of Aslan, the king, and went to bow in cat form when she felt the sharp prick of a knife in her leg. She roared a growl that shook the trees and transformed at the feet of the man she had only meant to pay her respects to.

Before she could speak a very tall man picked the one who had stabbed her up by the scruff of his neck and shook him like a rag doll before tossing him away like garbage. He approached her and her gaze was fixed on him. She felt the king kneel behind her, heard him ask if she was okay but she could only watch the man before her.

"May I?" he asked and held his hands above her wound. She could feel the burn of her flesh and muscle and she nodded thinking he meant to check her wound. Instead he held his hand over her flesh and closed his eyes. A heat seemed to move from him to her and with amazement she watched and felt as her wound began to heal and repair.

"You are a healer?" the king Aslan spoke the question.

The man waited until he was through, until she was completely healed before standing and answering. And still he held a hand out to her to help her to her feet. "I am Micah. I am Danuja. And, yes, I am a healer."

"What brings you to our lands?" queried Aslan.

"I came to bring you word of a plot," Micah answered and Lynx was not surprised when everyone moved closer to him. "It seems that there is someone who is not happy with their king and seeks to have him killed."

"Is that so," Aslan smiled and it was absolutely feral, a grin to do a shifter proud.

"Yes," Micah nodded. "And I come in search of my brother who disappeared from your shores over a year ago. Though knowing what my own fate was to be by this man named Wilhelm, I fear I may be too late."

"And what has Wilhelm to do with you?" Aslan asked, a frown marring his brow. It was a question that Lynx wanted the answer to as well.

"He was to be burned at the stake for simply existing," Aurora spoke before laying her hand on Micah's back. "If your brother lives then we will find him."

Micah nodded and took in the protective stance of the two men behind her. "I see your mates found you as you said."

She laughed and there was pure joy in the sound and on her face. "Yes, I only wonder what took them so long."

The fairer skinned of her mates grinned at that and pulled her close to his side leaning down for a kiss that quickly turned passionate. It was something to see a love that intense. The darker skinned one just stood behind them, his gaze watching everyone and everything. It was easy to see that she would be protected from this moment on. And it was this man that he approached.

"I owe your mate my life," he said and bowed to the shorter man. "I have taken a vow of protection unto her. I will guard her with my life."

The dark man nodded and the other man turned and nodded as well, Aurora still in his arms. "It will be an honour to accept your guard. I am Domi and this is Nado. We thank you for helping our mate."

Micah laughed as much at his words as at the punch Aurora threw his way. "'Twas she that saved me," he stated and bowed at the shoulders to her.

"As we knew she would," Nado stated.

"Thank you for healing my sister," Aurora said to him.

Micah bowed again from the shoulders.

"It seems we have much to sort and discuss," Aslan said. "All of which would be easier done with food and drink. Why don't we head to my home?"

Micah, Lynx, Domi and Nado all looked at Aurora who nodded her head. It was time to find some answers and perhaps discover new questions.

Chapter Four

The room was beautiful. Aslan hadn't even batted an eye when Domi suggested that they be shown to their room first. He'd just said that was a good idea and that they could all meet in an hour to discuss things. She had many questions for him. Many. But first she would have to deal with her mates. She would have to watch her volume though. Micah was directly across the hall from them and Lynx was right next door. Obviously they all knew what was going to take place in this room but she didn't have to provide sound.

As soon as Nado shut the door Aurora found herself airborne and landing on her back on a very large bed in the middle of the room. Domi pounced on her and leaned in to claim her lips. The kiss was commanding, taking, possessing. It was as if he needed so much from her in that moment and it was then that she realised just how worried he had been.

"You will go nowhere without one of us at your side from now on," he commanded as he pulled back to gaze down at her.

He was good but not that good. She just grinned and shook her head. "No."

"Yes," he demanded.

"Domi, I love you but I will not consent to such treatment. You have seen me fight and had I a weapon on me when they showed up we would not be here now." She reached up to caress his face wanting to reassure him even as she denied him. "I will promise to always be with my sword. Where I go it will go as well. I cannot stop you from following me but I can ask you to trust me. I have done nothing to lose that."

Domi leaned low, his forehead touching hers. "I cannot bear to lose you again, even for a moment. When we found out you were gone it was as if a knife had speared straight into my heart. I would be lost without you. You are my everything."

"Domi," she whispered awed by his words. "Don't you know that I feel the same about you? But I cannot be with you every moment of every day. I am just learning who I am. Now I must find out why I was taken and what my role is within these walls. There will be people here who will tell me more of my mother. And it appears that I have a twin brother to get to know."

"You are twins?" Nado queried as he joined them on the bed. She knew he had secured the room giving Domi a chance to hold her and reassure himself. "You look much alike. Hair colour, eye colour and shape, the stubborn tilt of your jaw and even some of the same facial expressions. Definitely siblings but I had no idea you were twins."

"So he says," she replied. "And there is much I must speak with him about," she looked at Domi as she finished, "alone. I will hold nothing back from you, this I swear. But some things I must learn by myself. And you must trust me to do that."

Domi let out a deep breath and she knew he was going to give in to her. He would still worry about her though, and only time would assure him. "I will try my love," he swore and that was good enough for her for now.

"I've missed you," she said nuzzling up into him and licking her way across his neck before nipping along his chin to his mouth. "Show me how much you've missed me," she purred.

Domi laughed and it was such a joy to see that she giggled with relief. They would be okay. "Come here you little minx," he murmured and moved deftly to roll them away from Nado so that he was beneath her. She sat up to straddle his thighs and reached for the hem of her shirt lifting it clear and tossing it carelessly to the side.

"Hmmm..." Domi said eyeing her as his hands ran down her stomach to the top of her leathers. "I'm glad we brought you several new pairs of these."

"Why is that?" she laughed but it was cut short when he grabbed the material and with a sharp tug ripped it wide open. She noticed the hint of cat claws on the tips of his fingers and shook her head. "No fair, cheating."

It was Domi's turn to laugh. "All is fair with a shifter."

Her leathers were shredded and thrown aside. She lifted up to undo his pants when she was almost knocked off balance by Nado removing her shoes. She glanced back to see him already naked, his cock curving up to his belly, and she knew what they were about to do.

"We won't hurt you," Nado promised.

"I know," she whispered, as shoeless, she went back to releasing Domi's cock.

Nado moved from the bed to one of the bags they had brought with them and removed a small tube. She knew what it was, had heard others mention it. It was simply called "the oil of love" by the shifters. It was oil that helped prepare a woman to take her mate anally. It softened and wet the tissues there while stroking the nerves and making the woman crave what was to come. She had no idea how it was made but she looked forward to experiencing it for the first time.

Before he could reach the bed she moved down Domi's body so that her head was even with his lap and her knees were close the bottom edge of the bed. She glanced back and saw Nado grin as he walked to her. This position would give him better access to her. But instead of the oil she got his tongue stroking through her slit from pussy to ass then back again where he twirled around her clit before sucking it into his mouth. She cried out and arched her back further allowing him deeper access. He was good, so incredibly good, that she was already close to orgasm.

She needed to focus on something else so she bent low to take Domi's cock into her mouth. He groaned and clenched his fingers into the covers beneath them. His taste was just as she remembered it, hot and salty. She ran her tongue over the head pressing it inside just a bit to make sure she had all of his cream that was already leaking from the slit. One hand was wrapped around him, only managing to hold half his width and so thick that he stretched her mouth wide, just as soon he would stretch her pussy.

She placed her hand at the bottom of his shaft using the other to fondle and squeeze his balls. Slowly she lowered her mouth down his shaft until her lips brushed her knuckles. He groaned and so did she sending the vibration of her sound up along his rod and making him cry out. She sucked his flesh hard as she lifted her mouth, stopping when only the head was inside, swirling her tongue over and around before taking him deep once more. Back and forth she moved until she had a rhythm going that worked for them both. She would go fast then slow it down and her strong panther was putty in her hands.

Then Nado slipped the first oiled finger into her ass. She cried out as much at the invasion as the immediate effects of the oil. She released Domi with a pop and tossed her head back and forth. One finger became two and soon she was leaning back into him riding the digits as she moaned and begged for more.

"She is ready," Nado said and his voice sounded strained.

Domi reached down and pulled her back up to straddle him lifting her hips so that she was balanced over his cock. She reached down to hold him at her opening and slid her pussy over his thick flesh. *So good, so fucking good.* How had they ever managed to wait so long to mate? When she would have begun to ride him he pulled her forward placing one hand on her hip to hold her flush against him. He was so hard and deep within her that it was torture.

"Just hold still for a moment, my love," he told her. "Let Nado join us so that you can see what it truly means to have two mates, how it is to form the perfect triad."

"Yes," she whispered and unable to hold still she began to lick and nip and suck every inch of Domi's flesh that she could reach, driving him as wild as her.

"Hurry," he encouraged Nado.

And then finally Nado was there. She could feel him tuck the head of his cock against the snug hole of her anus. But there was so much oil. They were both slick with it.

And his entry was not as uncomfortable as it could have been. The oil really was magical. He popped through that first tight ring of muscle and slowly moved forward until he was all the way in, his balls flush against her.

She cried out with the burning pleasure of it. She was full, so full that she felt as if one stroke from either man might split her in two. She wanted to move, to adjust, to alleviate the immense pressure in some way but their hands held her still.

"Please," she tried to cry but her mouth was suddenly dry and the word came out as a whisper.

She managed to wiggle just a bit and both men groaned and finally began to move. She wanted to scream at first just from the pure intensity of what she felt. Every inch of her body was alive. Every nerve involved in this act of possession and love. She had nothing to compare this to. It was the most intense moment of her life, better than anything she had known before. Each thrust seemed to wake new sensations, new emotions within her.

It was a rhythm that had one entering while the other withdrew. She had no time to recover from the sensations that one gave her before she was forced higher by the other. No slow build here, only sensation after sensation that had her flying ever higher. Orgasm this way just might kill her. Surely her body couldn't take much more. That is what she thought until the rhythm changed and they began thrusting and retreating together. She was full, so full then empty.

She came with a scream that must have reached every member of the house if not all those in the countryside around them. Her body trembled, her muscles burned and she thought she just might pass out. She felt Domi tighten beneath her, felt the harsh blast of his seed and still Nado kept going. One, two, three more hard strokes and he was with them, coming with a cry to rival her own and filling her ass with his hot fluid.

They collapsed in a pile of limbs on the bed and somehow the men moved so they lay on their sides. Nado was still in her ass, though Domi had slipped free of her pussy. She just needed to sleep for a moment. She closed her eyes and let the smile touch her lips. She was the luckiest woman in the world.

She'd left them again to go and speak with family. She almost laughed at how mad Domi would be. But Nado would expect it of her. She grinned like a fool. They really were all perfect together. But this was something she needed to do. She needed to speak with her brother, with Aslan, and maybe find out things she didn't know. It was hard to adjust to the idea of having a brother, much less a twin. It would definitely take some getting used to.

She found herself in a long hallway filled with paintings. One called to her. The woman in it looked a lot like her and it wasn't hard to figure out that this was her mother. The hair, the eyes, it was her, only slightly older. Her mother had been softer or at least appeared so in the portrait. And the sword that even now hung from a sheath at Aurora's side was included in the portrait.

"She was an amazing woman," a deep voice came from behind and to the right.

Aurora turned one hand on the hilt of her sword to see an older man there. He was tall and still well muscled but had a soft smile on his lips as he gazed at her mother's image.

"You loved her?" she asked but she could see the answer in his face.

"Everyone did," he replied finally moving his eyes to her. "She was quite a woman, one of a kind."

"I never got the chance to know her," she said and moved her gaze back to the picture.

"Lydia was her nursemaid," he supplied. "When your mother was murdered she stole you away in the night leaving your brother at the mercy of whoever found him."

"She did what was asked of her," Aurora stated with a smile. "And I grew up with her daughter so I did have a sibling."

"She was pregnant when she left," he said and she wasn't sure if it was a question or a statement.

"Yes, my sister Lynx was born just six months later. There is less than a year between us," Aurora said.

"She is the one that came with you?" he queried. "The shifter who can take many shapes?"

"Yes," she murmured growing a little leery now of his interest in her sister.

"She is very beautiful, as is her sister," he said and moved forward to stand beside her. She remained tense, one hand on her sword, though she couldn't place why she felt threatened by him.

"Yes, she is quite a fierce warrior in her own right," Aurora added.

"As her sister is as well," he said and let his glance fall to the sword at her side. "Your mother was too. She fought better than anyone I've ever seen. She was never without the sword you now carry. Until the night she died."

"She was unarmed?" she asked.

"She was coming to see me that night," he said. "We were to discuss important matters. But a woman I had held for questioning escaped and before anyone could stop her she had stabbed your mother and in the aftermath made her escape."

"Why was this woman held for questioning?" she queried.

"That is in the past," was all he would say before moving on. "You have her beauty, her blood. She was an amazing queen. You have much to live up to."

"Ahh…but then I never knew her so it is easy for me to be my own person and not a shadow of what I did not know," she replied and his eyes came up this time with a hostile glare in them. "And I don't know that I will stay to fulfil this role of queen."

"Yes," he agreed. "Perhaps you should take your leave before you upset the wrong person with your lack of respect."

"I see," she said. "We'll just have to see what my brother plans to do to persuade me otherwise."

"Aslan will always put the good of his people first," the man said. "He knows his place."

"We'll see," she said, somehow knowing that the words would get under his skin. She had become the enemy again over the course of their talk and suddenly she thought she knew exactly who she was speaking to.

"Does he know of the mates you keep company with?" he asked and there was disgust in his voice. Yes, he would be one who would not tolerate a mixing of magic. He would want her to mate within her own class and the warrior class was the ruling class.

"He knows and seems to have no issue with it," she said and took a few steps away from him. She made it look as if she wanted a closer look at the next portrait but in reality she just wanted distance. "Does he know of your little hobbies? Such as burning people at the stake? Kidnapping?"

"I don't know what ignorance you spout," his voice was hard, all traces of friendliness gone. "I have no hobbies outside of counselling the king."

"Really," she said and turned to face him. "Perhaps I shall stay for a while then. Just to get to know my brother of course."

He glared at her. Yes, an enemy. "Of course." And with a condescending bend of his shoulders he stiffly bowed and turned to walk away.

"It was nice to finally meet you Wilhelm," she called after him and other than a brief pause he just continued to walk away. "Very illuminating," she murmured as she turned back to the portrait of her mother. "What secrets did you take to the afterlife with you?" she asked. "What secrets does he hide?"

"I'd like to know the answers to those myself," a voice she recognised spoke from her left. She wasn't surprised to turn and see Aslan there. "Would you care to come in and talk?" he indicated the door behind him as he spoke.

"Yes," she said already moving towards him. "I think there is much we can share with one another." Something wasn't right. Wilhelm had been in love with her mother and from the look on his face still was. But there was guilt in his eyes as well and she didn't believe his story of a woman escaping and killing her mother. What she knew from Lydia didn't mesh with his tale. It was time to find answers. It was time to find the truth of how her mother died.

Chapter Five

"So what was it like for you?" Aslan asked her as he shut the door behind them. "Growing up among the shifters?"

So they were going to start with the get to know you stuff. She could do that. "It was great. It sucked. Fascinating. Irritating. Never a dull moment," she answered truthfully and couldn't cover the grin that tugged her lips.

"So you really did have a good childhood?" he asked.

"Yes," she assured him. "I really did. It was hard at first watching those around me find their guardian spirit and learn to shift and change. Especially hard when you have a sister that can shift into many forms while you can take none."

"That had to be difficult," Aslan said.

"It was until the first time I picked up a weapon," she smiled at the memory. "I must have been eight or nine. I was mad about something," she shook her head and laughed. "Some childhood wrong. I was storming away, mad as hell when I stumbled across an axe. I picked it up and it just felt right in my hand. I turned and began tossing it. I remember one of the men yelling for me to put it down. The shifters watching were scared."

"What happened?" he asked.

"Lydia came over and told them to leave me be," she shook her head. "And they did. I tossed the axe back and forth and finally turned and threw it. It landed in a tree in the exact spot I aimed for. It was exhilarating. I felt euphoric with a weapon in my hand. From that point on I found every weapon I could get my hands on and within minutes was an expert with them. It seemed to come from inside," she glanced up at him. "I had this knowledge inside me and just knew what to do."

"Yes," he nodded. "You are the queen's daughter. Warrior by birth. It is in your blood, a part of your soul."

She nodded saying nothing. She wasn't quite ready to admit to anything that might chain her permanently here. "Wilhelm thought perhaps I would be happier leaving," she said instead to see what Aslan would say.

He was not happy. "Our uncle has no say in that. Besides, you cannot leave," and when she just arched her eyebrow at him he added, "not yet anyway. Please. We need a chance to get to know one another." He turned and headed across the room to a little cart that held glasses and a dark drink that she didn't recognise. He poured two glasses and brought one to her before sipping at his own. He seemed suddenly agitated.

"It was different for you," he said. "You did not know of me. She didn't tell you of me." He looked at her and there was such anguish in his eyes. "But I have always known of you, searched for you from the time I was old enough. No, probably before I was really old enough. Searched and failed. My sister. My other half. I felt empty and alone in ways that none could understand. Even you it seems." And he seemed so sad by that. It touched her deeply and made up her mind.

"I felt those same things," she told him. "I felt alone and empty, as if there was this void inside that just couldn't be filled." Her turn to sip at the liquid and she almost coughed as the fiery substance burned all the way down her throat to her belly. Warmth built and spread and she decided that she liked it. "But I was with people who were not my own. I couldn't be like them no matter how hard I tried. So I thought that was what it was. I didn't know about you and the more I learn the more I am sure that was to protect me as well."

"Protect you from your own brother?" he sneered at the idea and she got a closer glimpse of the pain he had suffered.

"From elements that have yet to be discovered by either of us," she answered. "I can feel it even now," she placed her hand over her heart. "In my heart, in my soul. There are things we don't know. But I think the time has come for us to find them out together."

"What things?" he asked and she wondered just how much Wilhelm had bent Aslan to his way of thinking without Aslan even knowing it.

"How do you feel about my mating with shifters?" she asked instead.

He looked confused for a moment. "You are happy, yes?" he asked. "They are good to you?"

"Yes," she smiled. "They are everything to me."

"Then I have no issue with them," he answered and she could read the honesty in him. So Wilhelm had not given Aslan his bigotry. "I saw how fiercely protective they were. I could ask no more than that for my blood."

She nodded. "I will stay," she held up her hand when he whooped and moved to hug her. "But only as long as I feel I need to. There are things here that I need to understand, that we both need to." He nodded and she was willing to bet that he would agree with anything right now just to make sure she stayed. "But first I'd like you to tell me about the role of queen and what this sword really means."

"Gladly," he said and pointed to two chairs. "Let's get comfortable," he held his glass up and pointed to hers. "More?"

She glanced down to realise her glass was empty. She didn't remember drinking it. That was not good. She could already feel the buzz in her skin, the warmth of the alcohol in her blood. She had never been much of a drinker preferring berry juice or the crisp clean taste of water. She shook her head no and took a seat as he refilled his cup. She needed a clear head to discuss this. The people now thought of her as queen whether she wanted the role or not. It would be best if she knew what that meant.

"Do you know much of the history of our people?" he asked her.

"I know that the warriors came and took over," she replied acerbically. "That we came and conquered what did not belong to us. That we forced the natives into hiding and that there was a time when we tried to use the shifters as slave labour."

"A stilted view but unfortunately accurate," he acknowledged. "There was a time when that was practiced. But then all cultures and races come with good and bad elements. It just seems that history reflects the negative more often."

She nodded and he relaxed back into his chair.

"The sword was originally from this land. It was the weapon of a native, embedded in her skin as is common with their people. She married outside her class, a foreigner that her people hated and attempted to kill. But their love was strong and in the end all they managed to do was drive her away. This was a tragedy for them as she was the last of their royal family. Her parents were older and had never been gifted with another child. She and her husband, who had no magic known to these lands, left and moved to a more central part of the country. He may not have had magic as the natives define it but what he did have was the ability to wield any weapon that came to hand with a mastery that defied logic. He was masterful. They were gifted with a beautiful daughter. But she was more like her father than her mother and her skin did not form the magic of the native people. And with them a new class of people grew and formed. The warrior."

"So the warrior class found its beginning here with a native princess?" she asked. "If true, that is a link which cannot be denied."

He nodded and continued the story. "Yes. And in the meantime her parents were gifted with another child, another girl. She grew strong and her weapons were mighty indeed. She became the hope of her people. And the child who had left grew sick. Her husband and her friends could not help her and as she lay dying she begged her husband to take her home one last time. Though it could mean his life, her man loved her enough to do anything. He was captured as they entered the village and separated from her. The people blamed him for her condition. She met her sister and spoke with her. When she asked for her husband there was silence."

"What happened? Oh my goddess," she exclaimed. "They killed him! Even knowing what he meant to her?"

"It wasn't her family for although they loathed him, they loved her more and would not do anything to hurt her. It was never them that tried to kill her husband, but another. There was a man within the tribe that had been betrothed to her and when she ran off with her warrior he killed himself. And it was his family that held the grudge."

"No," she whispered.

"While her family was surrounding her they killed her husband where he was tied and unable to defend himself." He leant forward and handed her a slip of cloth. It was then that she felt the tears on her face. "With her dying breath, the native princess weaved a spell that none had ever seen before. She said that when she died her sword would leave her flesh and go to her daughter. This would be the sword that ruled the land and all would bow in its presence. It would pass through her bloodline from daughter to daughter for all time."

Aurora looked at the sword at her side and was awed by the power she held. "My sword?"

"Your sword," he agreed. "Now she loved her family and didn't want them to fade away. So what she said was that they would be cursed to walk in shadow never calling one place home."

"Never?" she asked recalling how Rory and her people were nomadic, how they seemed to disappear before your very eyes.

"Well the legend says that she did tell them that they would be given one more chance. A daughter would be born and she would fall in love with a warrior greater than they had ever known. And that when the two lines merged once more with the blessing of their people all would be well and they would once more find home." He sat back and smiled at her. "You must have loved hearing stories as a child. I'm sorry that I missed that." He looked so sad that it made her heart break.

"I'm sorry for that loss as well," she grinned. "For you can tell one hell of a story, brother." It was a slip of the tongue, an unconscious word that seemed natural to use but hearing it lit Aslan's face in a way that made her glad that she had said it.

"It is a powerful weapon you hold, sister," he told her. "With it you rule at my side, my right hand so to speak. While I deal with the politics and the mental challenges, while I decree and pass judgement, you are the weapon that sees it carried out. You are the one that is feared and revered. You are the warrior of the people."

It was a lot to take in. She was only just realising the enormity of what lay ahead for her, for her mates and for all the people. She was only just coming to the knowledge that they would not leave, not permanently. This was her home, her destiny and now she understood why Lydia had tried to keep her separate from Domi and Nado. To protect them all from what was bound to happen. For her home was now inside these walls and a shifter needed open space. How was she going to work this out with her mates?

"I see your mind working," Aslan spoke as he stood. "I'll leave you to your thoughts and head off to my bed. I'd suggest you do the same. Tomorrow will be a big day for you."

"Why is that?" she queried.

"Tomorrow you will be officially introduced to the people as their queen."

"Why tomorrow?" she asked feeling a little touch of panic at the idea. "Shouldn't we wait a while?"

He smiled at her. "Word of your amazing entrance has already spread. People are already showing up to see their queen, to glimpse her and see if she is the warrior they hoped and prayed for. They have waited a long time for you," he leaned in and kissed her cheek before pulling back and brushing his fingers over the same spot. She knew that he was thinking of how long he had waited as well. "They will be denied no longer. You belong to the people now. Welcome to my world." There was a touch of sadness in his voice that she wondered at.

"I belong to no one," she stated instead. "I may be queen by birth. I may be mated to two of the greatest men in the world. I am sister, friend, lover. But when I face the day I know who I am. I am Aurora. A woman. A warrior. And now a queen. But when night comes I am still just me and I belong to none but those I choose. A choice brother. And no one gets to make it but me."

"I envy your strength of conviction," he said as he headed to the door. "And I pray that it lasts."

It would last. It would have to. You could only be who you were and believe that was enough. She would not lose herself for anyone or anything. She may have grown without her mother but she had always felt a strength and guidance within that she was coming to believe was her mother. Her blood was strong. Her courage was great. And her confidence was immeasurable. If there was a way to make everything in her world mesh and flourish, she would find it. After all she was queen.

Domi was the only one in the room when she made it back and he did not look happy to see her.

"If you don't stop glaring at me I'm going to turn around and walk right back out the door," she muttered as she shut the door and crossed the room towards him.

He met her half way and took her into his chest with a firm grip on each shoulder. "If you do not stop leaving before Nado and I wake then I will tie you to our bed," he stated as he continued to squeeze her.

"Now that sounds like fun," she whispered placing kisses over every inch of him she could reach.

"I'm not joking Aurora," he said using his hold to put a little bit of distance between them. "You have to start including us in your little trips, or at least letting us know where you are going and why you must do it alone."

She could have gotten angry. He was being dominating, controlling. But honestly he wasn't being either. He was just a man in love, afraid for his woman. And it made her love and respect him even more because he wasn't angry with her. He was just asking her to include him, something she would demand from him.

"I will," she promised. "I swear to you that I will not leave again without telling you. No matter the circumstance."

He looked at her and must have seen the truth in her eyes for finally he pulled her close again and hugged her. "I love you little warrior. More than anything else in this world."

"I love you too Domi," she whispered. "Now take me back to that big bed and show me."

With a sweep of his arms she was cradled high against his chest and he was doing just that. He set her beside the bed and slowly undressed her, caressing and rubbing against every inch of newly exposed skin. He had her writhing before her pants hit the floor. He was still wearing his pants when he laid her out on the bed before him. She spread her legs wide for him wanting to feel his mouth on her flesh there. And Domi didn't disappoint her.

His dark head lowered and there was just something erotic about the black of his skin against the pale cream of her thighs. His coal eyes held her gaze as his fingers spread her pink lips and that wicked tongue flashed out to draw through her opened flesh. He was good, so fucking good. She wanted to close her eyes but the desire to watch him was too strong to deny.

He ran his tongue in and out of her pussy, using it like a small cock to fuck her. She undulated beneath him, couldn't stop her hips from rising up to him. He grinned that wicked grin at her, the one that made her melt.

"Please," she begged wanting him to stop playing and make her come.

She watched his eyes flash, saw his nose quiver in that way that was so unique to a shifter and he finally dove in, driving screams from her as he devoured her pussy. Lips, teeth and tongue, he used them all with wicked intensity against her. She came and still he worked her higher drawing out her orgasm and bleeding it into another and yet another. Still he worked that tongue against her clit while pumping two fingers in and out hitting her sweet spot with every stroke.

"Domi," she cried out. "Fuck me. Fuck me now before I die from this pleasure."

"Gladly," he said and pulled back to stand on the floor beside the bed.

Aurora watched with lust as he stripped the leathers from his legs. He was so powerful even in his human form. With his dark skin it was easy to imagine him as the panther that lived within him. Part animal, part man, and all hers. He reached down and ran his palm over his cock and she felt her mouth water for a taste of him. So thick and already there was a little drop of cream waiting there on the tip for her.

She moved to her knees then onto all fours so that her mouth was even with his cock. She wanted him, had to have him and he was making no move to stop her. She opened wide and sucked the head into her mouth taking him all the way in until her lips bumped against where his fingers were wrapped around the stalk. Back and forth she moved sucking and licking. His taste drove her crazy made her crave more. She loved the little notch just under the head. She especially liked the way his eyes darkened and his dick jumped in her mouth when she made a point of rubbing her tongue there.

His other hand came up to grip her head and soon it was anyone's guess if he was fucking her mouth or she was fucking him with her mouth. Their rhythm was so in sync that it was hard to tell just who had the control. She pulled back so that just the crown was in her mouth and he held her there, unwilling to let her move back down his shaft. So she sucked harder, worked her tongue from notch to slit and used her teeth to scrape the top of his shaft just under the head.

With a growl he pulled free and for the first time she could see the cat in his face as he fought to stay man and not turn into beast. It was exhilarating to know that she could break his control to that point. He used his hands to move her and she found herself on her hands and knees facing away from him. He pulled her back so that her knees slipped off the bed and settled on the tops of his thighs. She glanced back. He was bent down a bit taking the brunt of her weight and lining them up so that his cock was right there.

With a hard thrust he was deep inside her and she screamed once more. His eyes were the golden glow of the panther and she was unwilling to turn from that gaze. He was beautiful, the most beautiful thing she had ever seen. His cock speared in and out of her pussy making every nerve in her sheath scream with pleasure. This was her man, her mate, her lover and best friend. He and Nado were so deep inside her soul that she would never be able to live without them.

She came and her legs burned with the effort to hold her hips up for him to keep fucking her. But Domi seemed to know. He let her legs slide down so that her feet settled on top of his. He leaned over her on the bed, one hand on her hip and the other wrapping around one of hers. His strokes slowed and she felt his breath on her neck.

"I love the way you smell when we love," he whispered. "It is the sweetest smell in the world. Your skin seems to soak in the love and release it as a bouquet of delight."

She was awed by his words. Domi was the dominant, the aggressive, not the sweet talker. And yet here, in this moment she saw more of him than she ever had. It brought tears to her eyes and made her realise that there was no fear left inside her of them being unable to work something out to allow her to stay within these walls. She was his soul as well and he would find any way to keep them together. She loved him so much that it hurt.

"I love you, Domi," she said and squeezed her fingers around the hand that was holding hers.

"My world, Aurora," he said. "You are everything that is good and pure in my world."

His strokes came a little faster, a little harder and soon she was climbing to a peak that she didn't think was possible. She arched her hips up just a little pushing them back towards him to deepen the angle of his thrusts. She was coming and it was almost like a thousand needles under her skin but needles that were giving her a drug that made her tingle and moan. The pleasure and pain were so meshed that it blurred the line so that even pain became pleasure.

He came with a feral roar behind her and she would swear that she felt the soft fur of the panther's skin for just a moment against her flesh. With a smile she turned to kiss him where he rested against her shoulder.

His eyes were lazy, his skin slick with the sweat of their loving. And still he was beautiful. In that moment she realised that she really did have no regrets about being the twin that was taken away and raised elsewhere. She had worried that the more she learned maybe she would. But she was happy. She was loved and cherished. It made her sad for her brother. She had seen the loneliness in his eyes and vowed to see them sparkle more often with the happiness he showed when she was around. He deserved to find what she had. But until he found it she would do everything she could to make him laugh and learn to see the fun in life. It was time she made up for all they had missed by growing up apart. She would give him a taste of what Lynx had done to her and show him what little sisters were for.

Chapter Six

Nado left the room laughing while Domi paced like a caged cat. He would give Domi some alone time with their mate. He had some other things he wanted to find out. His first stop was to check on Lynx and make sure that she was healing okay and staying out of trouble. He'd seen the way she looked at the Danuja, Micah. It was the same look that Aurora used to send to him and Domi. Once he made sure Lynx was behaving he would go talk to Micah. He had some things he wanted to know and unlike the others he wasn't content to wait.

But Lynx was missing from her room. The little cat would be hard to keep track of in a place with this many rooms. The way that she had looked at Micah he just might find his mate's sister where she shouldn't be. He hurried his steps up as he went across the hall to Micah's door.

The Danuja answered immediately and Nado pushed in and scanned every inch of the room. No one else was there.

"Can I help you find something?" Micah asked and Nado felt short next to the giant of a man. But for all his outward strength it was easy to sense the calm that seemed to surround Micah. Even when he had been upset when Lynx was stabbed he had merely picked the man up and tossed him aside. It would have been very easy for Micah to kill the man with his bare hands.

"I was seeing if perhaps Lynx was in here with you,' Nado said. "She was not in her room."

"I fear she has probably scampered off to cause some new form of mischief," Micah sighed and Nado laughed. The guy already had a handle on Lynx.

"I'm sure you are right," Nado agreed.

"So what is the other reason that you have come to my door?" Micah asked.

"Aurora says that you were to be burned at the stake?" he queried and Micah nodded. "Yet, I have a feeling that you knew that this was a possibility should you come to these shores."

"Yes, we have heard of the terror of Wilhelm's men on our shores as well," Micah admitted.

"Yet you came anyway." It was a statement and not a question.

"Yes, I did," Micah acknowledged. "My people have knowledge of a plot to rid your people of their king. An emissary was sent from us six months ago in hopes of reaching King Aslan and warning him. He was the best of our people and he never returned."

"Your brother," Nado sighed now understanding why Micah would offer to come next.

"My twin brother," Micah said and Nado's head whipped up.

"A lot of twins popping up all of a sudden," Nado said and wasn't surprised when Micah laughed.

"Not so sudden for me," Micah said. "I have known my twin since birth and until six months ago we have always been together."

"Are his talents the same as yours?" Nado asked.

"No," Micah said. "His are uniquely his own. I read people, the colours that surround them and know if they are lying, if they are healthy or near death."

"So you can tell if someone is good or bad?" Nado asked.

"We are all both at any given moment," Micah explained. "I only know if you lie when you speak."

"And you can heal?" Nado remembered well how he had used only his hand to heal the wound on Lynx's lower leg.

"Yes, I am a mender," Micah nodded. "Both skills which will make me a good personal guard for your queen."

"My mate," Nado corrected with a grin. "My woman, but not my queen."

Micah just looked at him and nodded.

"So is there a bond between you and your brother that would allow you to know if he were dead? If he were alive?" Nado switched topics.

"Yes," Micah answered. "He is alive though weak at the moment. His life slips slowly but I will find him before it is too late."

"You can see that?" Nado asked.

"No," Micah's golden eyes seemed to glow. "It is a vow that I intend to keep. His gifts will keep him strong until I find him."

"What are his gifts?" Nado was curious enough to ask.

"While I can heal others, he can heal himself," Micah said.

"And is that the only gift that your brother has?" Nado queried further.

"No," was the only answer Micah gave him.

"So do you have any idea where we should begin our search for your brother?" Nado planned to help this man who had been with Aurora in her moment of crisis. Micah's demeanour would have helped to calm her.

"Where Wilhelm hides is where I will find him," Micah said and Nado had to agree.

It seemed that all of the negative started and ended with Wilhelm. And this was the man who had raised Aurora's brother, Aslan, as his own. He would watch the man closely whether he was brother, twin or whatever. It would be hard to remain pure on a daily basis when touched by what Nado believed to be pure evil. It seemed that to find the answers to everything he would have to discover what he could about the elusive Wilhelm and pray he didn't lose his temper and kill someone. After all, this was the man who had intended to kidnap Aurora. Wilhelm would be lucky if Nado didn't hit him on sight.

"I have an idea of where to get more information on Wilhelm," Nado said and looked back at Micah. "Interested?"

"Yes," Micah stated and reached for a bag that he tied onto the belt at his waist. "It is best to know your enemy before you approach."

"Yes," Nado agreed and now it seemed like they all had a common enemy. Wilhelm.

Lynx was comfortable in her form as a small tabby cat. She took on the calico colour and was able to slink around wherever she wanted with little awareness of the people around her. Some would shoo her away. Some would offer her food or water. But none ever saw her as the threat that she was. People spoke freely around her, of everything and everyone so she had picked up a lot of gossip here among her sister's people.

Now she followed behind a woman carrying a tray down into the underground of the castle. She was being playful, swiping at the woman and weaving in and out of her legs while being careful not to trip her. But the young woman didn't know that.

"You foolish cat," the woman said. "You're going to trip me and then we will both be in trouble. I'll be sent to serve in ways that I have no desire to and you will be the next dish on this tray."

Lynx moved to the side and meowed as she continued at the woman's side.

"Hate coming down here anyway," the woman muttered. "Dark and dank and smells like death. No idea how many poor souls Wilhelm has brought down here, how many have died for no reason other than he wanted them to."

They finally reached the bottom of the stairs and headed down a dark corridor. So this was where Wilhelm kept that which he wanted to remain hidden. She would have to remember where the door was hidden in the kitchen pantry so that she could bring Micah and maybe Domi and Nado down later to look for Micah's brother.

"'Twould be for the better in my opinion if King Aslan learned of all this and Wilhelm was finally put in his place," the woman muttered then seemed to still as she realised that she had spoken out loud. "You will be the death of us both if I keep talking to you," she whispered to Lynx the tabby. "Best mind my own business and get this to the big one."

She continued down the hall taking turns here and there that Lynx prayed she could remember. Finally they stopped in front of what appeared a dead end.

"I know you are hidden here somewhere," the woman muttered as she sat the tray of food down. "I thank you for not hurting me," she squeaked and took off.

But Lynx did not follow. There was magic here and magic that she had never seen before. She could feel the ripple in the air like a thick blanket that cloaked the entire end of the corridor.

She almost peed when a hand appeared out of nowhere and she was lifted by the scruff of her neck.

"Well, what have we here?" a voice said and she was lifted against a massive chest, secure but not hurt by any means. "A pretty pussy to pass the time with."

Somehow those words sent a chill through her, as if the man holding her tabby form knew that she was more than a cat and that the petting he wanted was more towards her human form. She peered up at him and was shocked to see a face so similar to Micah's that this could be none other than his brother. The resemblance was to the point that if she did not know better she would swear it was Micah. Only this man was even taller than Micah's seven feet, broader of shoulder and yet not as strong on the inside as Micah. She remembered that he had been missing for a good six months at least. What exactly had Wilhelm been doing to this man?

"So what should I do with such a pretty little kitty?" he murmured and she meowed.

He laughed and the sound was deep and rich. His eyes were not quite as golden as Micah's. No, his eyes had dark brown flecks in them. His smile was just as warm and inviting though. His hair was longer but she didn't know if it was by choice or circumstance. Either way it looked really good on him. It was hard to judge from her position against his chest but it looked a long way down to the floor. She would bet he was at least an inch or two taller than Micah's seven foot frame.

Man she was as bad as her sister Aurora. Lynx had thought she had it bad for Micah but, hell, she was just as hot for his brother. Even as a cat she was content to lie snug against his chest. If he continued to stroke her with his fingers she just might sprawl and purr…after shifting back into human form. Lord, she just needed to have sex which was a laugh and a half.

The one time she had managed to sneak off with another shifter to learn what all the thrill was about she had only gotten so far before her wonderful mother had interrupted them. But before that interruption she had found out just how amazing it felt to have a tongue bath in all the right places. She had still been in the thrall of her first orgasm when her mother appeared. Mommy may have prevented her from popping the proverbial cherry but she hadn't prevented her from thoroughly enjoying the full extent of foreplay.

His fingers stroked along her fur again and she really wanted to know his name because heaven help her she was going to be moaning it soon.

He knelt down and placed her gingerly on the cool floor before standing and melding back into the shadows. She could feel him but could no longer see him. She wondered if that was some form of magic within him or within the place.

"Scamper home," he murmured far above her. "Before the boogey man shows and you never get away." His voice was sad now and hearing the change made her sad as well.

She took off back down the corridor letting her animal instincts direct her towards the fresh air above. She found her way to the door but had to sit patiently outside it scratching and meowing before it finally opened. The same woman from earlier greeted her with a pat and a reprimand.

"Finally find your way back, huh?" the woman said as she petted Lynx. "Lucky one aren't you. Best be off with you now before someone finds you in the kitchens. You've been gone for hours and hours. I'm sure someone must be missing you by now."

Shoot, Lynx thought. She'd had no idea she'd been down below for so long.

She took off as fast as her legs would carry her, heading for the stairs where she hoped Micah was in his room. She needed to tell him what she'd discovered on her tour of the castle. And then they could gather reinforcements and get the one Micah was searching for. She shifted as soon as she hit the door and was standing back in her clothed human form when it opened.

"I've news that you'll be excited to hear," she told Micah as she pushed by him into the room. "We need to gather the others and head out as soon as we can."

"What have you found little cat?" Micah asked and his voice made her just as wet as his brother's had. "Have you any idea of the time it is? We've been worried about you. Nado and I searched for you today outside the castle. You were nowhere to be found."

"I'm touched to know that you were concerned enough to look for me," Lynx said with a smirk. "But I've been taking care of myself for a long time."

"So your sister said," Micah nodded. "But still I worried. There is evil here that you should not face on your own."

"Aren't you even a little bit curious to know what I found today?" she queried bringing him back to the reason why she was here in his room to begin with.

"I've found your brother," she said with a grin. "Grab your stuff and let's go find my sister and her mates. I can get you back to where he is but I can't tell you what might stand in our way."

He stood and looked at her for a minute before dropping the lock on the door he'd just shut. His face was a plethora of emotions. Surprise, joy, anger, fear, apprehension, and amazement. She had no idea what path his mind was taking. But for the moment he seemed content to follow her lead.

"For tonight you can sleep here," he said pointing to the bed that she knew must still smell of him. "We will discuss your antics later," he promised. "And after a good night's sleep we will go speak with all the people who need to be involved in this. We must be smart and not rush in without the proper knowledge of what we face."

"What antics?" she asked curiously choosing to focus on the comment he made about her.

"This desire you have to run off on your own with no one aware of where you have gone," Micah told her.

"My life is my own," she whispered. "I will continue to do as I please."

"For now," was all he said but it was enough to make her fume. Who did he think he was? So she wanted to fuck him. Hell, she wanted his brother as well. And her mother wasn't here to stop her this time. But wanting sex did not mean mating and even if it did, her mates would not tell her what to do.

"What…" she began but he interrupted before she could finish.

"We will discuss it later, Lynx," he told her as he turned her towards the bed. "First we must rest and then you can tell us where to locate Merced. He was well when you saw him?"

As much as she wanted to tell him to go to hell she couldn't deny the anxiety in his eyes. She had the power to ease his worry and she would. "Yes, he seemed well when I saw him earlier."

He looked closely at her and she wondered what he was trying to see. Finally he must have found what he was searching for. He grabbed her hand and gave it a squeeze then kept it in his as he pulled her down to sit on the bed.

"I thank you Lynx," he murmured softly, "for finding my brother." She started to smile until he bent low so that his face was right in front of hers. His mouth stopped mere inches from hers. If she wanted she could lick his lips. And she wanted. Very badly. She thought maybe that was his intention. His eyes flicked to her lips and she couldn't resist using her tongue to wet them. His eyes flipped back to hers and he grinned. "And later, we will have that talk."

He straightened up before she could even catch her breath. He grabbed a blanket and pillow from the bed and moved across the room to make a bed in front of the door. She had no idea whether it was to keep her in or others out. Oh, they would talk all right. She'd definitely set the infuriating Danuja straight on a few things.

Chapter Seven

Aurora must have fallen very soundly asleep after the intense loving she had shared with Domi. She awoke to soft touches and the hard length of a curved cock against her sprawled thighs. Nado was between her legs, their hips snug. He held his upper body away from her with one arm braced on the bed by her head. The other hand he was using to slowly stroke over her skin. At the moment he was tracing increasingly smaller circles around her breasts growing closer and closer to her already turgid nipples.

"Touch them," she begged. "Don't tease me."

Nado laughed and bent his head to her. Starting at her shoulder he nibbled his way across and slowly made his way up the column of her throat. She writhed beneath him, moaning and begging for his touch, his caress. She could feel the pool of desire deep inside, feel the evidence of that desire coating the lips of her pussy as her body prepared to take him. She hoped it would be soon.

His lips were tracing the shell of her ear now, nibbling and sucking before sliding his tongue inside to trace. He pulled back and blew a breath of cool air and she felt her nipples tighten further, felt her sex clench around nothing.

"Nado, damn you," she demanded using her elbow to knock his arm off so that he fell to her chest and she finally felt a touch of friction against her breasts. She used her thighs to anchor his hips between hers pulling herself up to rub her cunt against his cock. "Stop fucking around and make us one."

He growled and it was as if there was a cat in the room with them, but they both knew it was the cat inside the man. His mouth possessed hers while his hands grabbed her hips and hiked her higher along his length. Then he rolled them so that she was on top of him.

"Take what you want," he said and grinned at her.

She moaned with delight. Trailing kisses down his jaw to his chest she used her hands to stroke every inch that she could touch. His nipples pebbled and she couldn't resist sucking and scraping them with her teeth. His moans mingled with hers and she delighted in the sound. She moved down to his stomach so rippled with muscle and used her tongue to trace every hard ridge. She could feel the damp trail that his cock left on her skin as she continued on her downward path.

Finally she straddled one hard thigh, her pussy rubbing up and down the hard length while she took the rock hard length she really wanted in her hands. Her mouth watered as she stroked her palms up and down his cock. She loved that wicked curve, loved that he was just a little bit longer than Domi. Honestly she just loved the way her man's cock felt when it was fucking in and out of her. Pussy, ass, or mouth didn't matter. She just loved sex with her mates.

She bent low over his cock teasing them both by how close her mouth was to that rounded head that already wept with desire. She closed her eyes and inhaled deeply enjoying the scent of him. Soon she would wear that again on her skin. It was erotic to her. She used her tongue to lick slowly over the very tip of his cock keeping her eyes closed and savouring the taste that filled her mouth. He was always so sweet on her tongue. She could lick him forever.

"You're killing me," Nado groaned and she opened her eyes to look up at him. She wondered what he thought of the view. She was angled above him. Her pussy tight against his thigh, her breasts dangling on either side of his delicious cock which she gripped between her palms. She knew her eyes were glazed with lust and pleasure, her lips still wet from him.

"Beautiful," he breathed as if reading her thoughts. "You are the most beautiful sight in this world we live in. I can never get enough of you."

"I feel the same for you," she whispered.

"But Aurora," his voice sounded strained. "If you don't suck or fuck soon, I won't be held responsible for my actions."

She laughed. Then she bent lower and sucked him into her mouth taking his cock as far into the back of her throat as she could. Her hand wrapped around what she couldn't consume and she began lifting and lowering her mouth along his flesh. She sucked and grazed her teeth taking pure pleasure in the sounds he made and the way his hips pumped up to meet her.

She worked her mouth faster, sucked harder. She wanted to taste him as he spilled inside her mouth. She wanted that hot blast of his semen on her tongue. So she worked for it doing every little thing she could think of to push him over the edge. The hand wrapped around his base rotated and squeezed and she used it in tandem with her mouth as she sucked. Her other hand moved lower to rub and caress his taut sac before she began to give it small tugs and squeezes.

"I'm going to come," Nado groaned. "I want to fuck you Aurora. I want to be inside you when I come."

She pulled her mouth away only long enough to say what she needed to. "You are inside of me. My mouth. And I want to swallow every hot, delicious burst of pleasure you give me." She glanced up at him unable to stop her tongue from reaching out to lick over his cock. "And then you can return the favour and we can start all over again." Her eyes lowered to the gorgeous cock she held in her hand. "I'm sure you're up to it." And then she consumed him sucking hard as she took him deep so deep that she could feel the head at the top of her throat. She swallowed. Once, twice being sure to breathe through her nose to counter the gag reflex that wanted to force him out.

And her man lost control. His fingers clenched tight in her hair and he held her close while he fucked her mouth. She used her mouth, hands, tongue and teeth to help him over that edge. He came with a roar that seemed to shake the walls around them. One harsh blast after another filled her mouth and she struggled to swallow it all. He tasted sweet, a perfect contrast to Domi's more salty taste. And she loved that, loved them.

His fingers loosened their grip and he used them to stroke slowly over her hair now. His breathing was laboured and she could feel his pulse where her head lay along the inside of his thigh by his groin. She let his cock slip from between her lips and licked the tiny dribble that still lingered at the slit in the head. He groaned and his body trembled beneath hers.

"Give me a few minutes, my love," he murmured. "Then I will pleasure you as well as you have me."

A few minutes sounded nice. Maybe she would recover from the orgasm she'd had when he exploded on her tongue. His pleasure had given her pleasure as well. Yeah, another few minutes to catch her breath and be ready for more. But Nado recovered more quickly and in just seconds he was moving out from under her.

She lay on her stomach, her head now nestled on the same spot his hips had rested, her knees bent to keep them on the bottom of the bed. He moved from the bed and around until he stood at the end. His hands came out to cup the heels of her feet and it tickled a little the way that he rubbed them. With him guiding her she rolled over to her back, her knees still tucked and bent close to her chest. She caught her breath at the look in his eyes as his glance fell to the pink slit of her pussy.

He lifted her feet and placed a kiss on the instep before placing them on top of his shoulders. He ran his fingers along the inside of her thighs spreading them while caressing each inch of her skin with his fingers and she shivered with anticipation. Closer and closer his fingers trailed a path to her cunt and her thighs began to quiver. The man might just make her come with a mere brush of his fingers.

He leaned into her, letting her legs slide down until her knees caught on his elbows. He braced his palms on the edge of the bed beside her buttocks and bent so that his mouth was centred right where she wanted it. He inhaled and his nose flared, his eyes darkened and a low rumble sounded from his chest. She couldn't imagine being mated to any man that wasn't a shifter. She liked the animal inside them, revelled in its fierce need and the way it would kill to protect what belonged to it. Her.

He ran his tongue along the slit of her sex tasting her, savouring her. His tongue circled the tip of her clit where it stuck out and moved back down. He dipped into her opening rimming it, before taking a leisurely stroke back to the top. She wanted to scream with the need that coursed through her body, while he was taking his time.

"Please, Nado," she whispered. "I want you so much that it's killing me."

"And you'll have me," he promised and she could hear the need he felt as well. "As soon as I gorge myself on you."

And finally he dove in, one hand moving to part her plump lips and fully expose her to him. He flattened his tongue against her and rubbed it from her opening to the now fully exposed bud of her clitoris. His tongue stayed there flicking and stabbing at the morsel before his lips closed over it and he sucked it deep. Her hips bucked off the bed and the scream did leave her lips. His name. It was all she could think at the moment. He completely consumed her, body, mind and soul.

"I love it when you call my name," he rasped and slid his other hand up to her cunt. He used two fingers to rim her hole before plunging them deep inside her. His lips tightened once more around her clit and now he pumped his fingers as well. She was going to explode, or maybe implode. All she knew was that she couldn't survive the intense pleasure much longer.

"Nado," she screamed his name again and again and a third time before she finally felt the tension unravel, the sweet release of orgasm. Only it was anything but sweet. It was hot and hard and all-consuming. Every inch of her skin throbbed and burned. Her knees clenched around his elbows and she used it to press her cunt higher so that his mouth was buried in her flesh.

She could feel the grin against her skin and if she hadn't been so boneless she might have swatted at him. Then again the man knew how to enjoy a good meal so why smack him for that? Instead she smiled as well while her body still shivered and trembled in the aftermath.

"Still want me?" he whispered as he inched up onto the bed using her position draped over his arms to ease her up further on it as well. He had them all the way back to the top of the bed and she still hadn't answered. "Aurora?" he asked and she could hear the laughter in his voice.

She did smack him this time but it was a weak attempt as her body was still feeling boneless and sated. And she only succeeded in making him laugh. He dropped her legs so that they were to the sides of his knees now and he looked down at her with pure love. She was indeed a very lucky woman.

"Am I breathing?" she queried.

"What?" he shook his head as if she were not making sense.

"Because that is the only thing that could possibly make me not want you," she answered and his eyes darkened again.

"I love you," he whispered and used one hand to guide his hard cock to her pussy. He pushed it inside with one slow thrust and rested there with their hips pressed tightly together. "I will love you every moment of my life and even death will not take that from us."

She felt the tears gather in her eyes and knew when they spilled over by the way he bent to lick them from her cheeks. Nado had been her best friend for as long as she could remember. Even before Domi had completed their circle, there had always been Nado.

She lifted to him and took his mouth with hers in a kiss that was meant to convey what words never could. He made love to her, slow and sweet.

"I love you too," she vowed. "And even when the goddess decides that my time is done, my love will remain. No matter which of us crosses first, no matter the roads that might make us part no matter how briefly. I will be yours and in the moments when you need me most, you will always find me in the warmth of your heart. Always."

His smile was warm and if she saw a little shine of unshed tears in his eyes she would never tell him. They loved. And no matter what roads lay ahead she and Domi and Nado would have that love to hold them close. And sometimes love was the greatest shield a person could wield.

Merced sat against the wall appearing asleep to anyone who might be able to see through the veil. He was alive. Still. But only because Wilhelm had not figured a way to drain his powers from him yet. If that day ever came Merced knew that he would die.

Wilhelm kept him behind these invisible walls. He could step out if he chose but only so far. He hated these walls and yet they were what kept him alive. Wilhelm wanted his power but even that desire wouldn't keep him alive if he wasn't controllable. Wilhelm couldn't take his powers but he could keep Merced from fully tapping into them. Otherwise the old man would lie dead beneath his feet even now.

Merced had come on a mission to let the king Aslan know that there was talk, rumours, of Wilhelm wanting the throne for his own. But it appeared to Merced that Wilhelm already had most of the power anyway. The man could obviously do what he wanted. He'd heard the girl that brought his food to him speak to the cat and say that she wished Aslan would discover what Wilhelm did down here. So it appeared that Aslan was king in name only. If he could get free, if he could find the key to escape then he would find this Aslan and shake some knowledge into him. If not then there was no way to contain Wilhelm's corruption to this island, no way to keep it from spreading out to the others. Wilhelm was a man that thirsted for power, hungered for full control. If it took his last breath he would see Wilhelm fall.

He wondered if the little kitty had been discovered yet. He had easily sensed that she was more than she seemed. He wondered if the lovely pussy would shift into a beautiful woman. He had little doubt that it would be so. Her smell had enticed him in a way that none of the women he had known ever had. He would have loved to have kept her down here with him, to make her shift so that he could lick the cream from her thighs. Instead he could only imagine.

"Sleeping Danuja?" The voice he had come to hate so well sneered out of the darkness into the shadows where Merced reclined against the wall. Wilhelm. Merced wondered what pain the man had in mind this eve. "Let's see if this will wake you up."

A throb of pain built inside Merced's chest and blossomed out until his entire body felt like it was on fire. He wanted to scream, wanted to buck and fight against the pain pulsing through his body. But he would not allow himself to. That would be to give Wilhelm pleasure and even in death Merced would deny the man that.

"No response," Wilhelm yelled and Merced could hear the sound of him slapping someone hard enough to echo off the walls. A feminine cry sounded. "Amplify your powers Danuja slut," he yelled. "Kill the bastard if you must. Just make him bleed."

She did what he said and Merced could feel the coat of sweat that began to rise on his skin as he fought against the increasing fiery flames. Not a flame that you could beat and extinguish. No these were flames that hid under the skin, that burned from the inside out, flames that only one of his people could wield. But she was weak, at least weaker than him at the moment. He wanted so badly to open his eyes and see if he could recognise her, see if he could place her among those that had gone missing from his tribe. But he could not do so, one wrong move and it would mean his death. So he kept his eyes closed, a look of sweet repose on his face, and fought with all he had inside.

"Enough," Wilhelm bellowed and there was the sound of flesh striking flesh again. He heard her fall, heard her cry out, and almost broke his silence. Only knowing that was what Wilhelm wanted kept him still and silent. He heard the harsh sigh and knew that Wilhelm no longer looked at him but was focused on the girl.

"You have disappointed me slut," Wilhelm stated and Merced used his keen hearing to mark every tiny movement the man made. "You know what happens when I am displeased." It wasn't a question and Merced felt his heart bleed at the terror that permeated from her.

"Please," she begged. "I'll do anything. I will try again." Sheer terror in her voice rocked him to his core. But by saving her he would be sacrificing not just himself but all people. He had to awaken Aslan and bring Wilhelm down. The king must be made aware of the corruption that reigned alongside him.

Wilhelm yelled something in a language that Merced did not recognise, but he heard the footsteps that approached and the voice that answered was almost as harsh and cruel as Wilhelm's.

"Take the slut and put her to good use for the rest of the eve," Wilhelm stated and Merced knew all too well what those words implied. She would be forced to service whatever of Wilhelm's personal guard that wanted her, perhaps even all of them.

"Please," she begged then gasped as the sound of rending clothing filled the air.

"Such ripe curves," Wilhelm's voice again. "They so enjoy a good fuck between your thighs. You were built to take a good hard fuck. Lush lips made for sucking as well as the ripe globes of your tits. All of that makes you the perfect little slut that you are."

Her cries filled the air again and from the sounds Merced knew that Wilhelm was touching those curves in such a way to cause pain. And yet the girl did not turn her power against Wilhelm. Merced would have sensed it if she had. So how was the vile man controlling her? He sensed no wards around her and yet she did nothing to protect herself.

Merced almost broke when he heard them dragging her screaming down the corridor. Almost. But his control was greater than Wilhelm could possibly imagine. He brought to mind the images of his family, his brother, his mother and father, his village of people, all depending on him. Sometimes sacrifices had to be made for the good of the people. Though it killed him inside, the pain burning hotter than the flames she had tried to use to break him, he held still and silent.

"Sleep well, Danuja," Wilhelm whispered and Merced had little doubt that the man knew that he was aware of what had just happened and that sleep would not come this eve. Harsh laughter filled the corridor as Wilhelm walked away and once again Merced contented himself with thoughts of murder. Wilhelm had best pray Merced stayed within the invisible prison. For freedom would bring death.

Chapter Eight

Aurora left early again, while both of her mates still slept, but this time she left them a note so they would know where to find her. She had no idea when Domi had returned and joined them. She remembered his kiss but that was all. She had woken this morning cocooned between them and had almost not been able to manoeuvre from her position in their joint embraces. Her men loved her and even in sleep had a need to touch her and assure themselves that she was within reach and safe.

Today was the day that her brother said she would be presented to the people as queen. She had been so wrapped up in that small fact that she had forgotten to ask him for further details. Like how, why and if there was something important that she should know beforehand. Leave it to her to face things unprepared. Good thing she didn't suffer from lack of confidence.

"My queen," a young girl curtsied and stayed low as Aurora passed her in the hallway.

"There is no need to bow before me," Aurora stated and used her hand to motion the girl up. The girl reluctantly rose and looked at Aurora. "I am queen by birth, by blood. But that makes me no more important than you or any other woman on this island or any other."

The girl smiled shyly and shook her head. "Forgive me my queen but there you are wrong. You are the best of us all."

Aurora shook her head as the girl turned to walk away. How was she to live up to such an illusion? She honestly was just herself, with her own unique gifts and talents. She could be no more or no less.

Several more people curtsied to her as she made her way to the room where she and her brother had spoken the night before. After the first two she no longer tried to tell them otherwise but only nodded and smiled at them. She wasn't sure that she would get use to it but one thing was sure. Her brother had said that word of her presence was already spreading and he was right. It seemed everyone now knew who she was. Then again maybe not.

She moved down the hall towards Aslan's office and was greeted by two armed warriors. Both were big and strong and not content to just let her pass by into the room undisturbed. They barred her saying that the king was in a meeting and she would wait. *Hell no,* was the thought that kept running through her head but there was no need to bother her brother when he was in a meeting. She would just wait and deal with where she was allowed or not, later. She was going to let it pass. Honestly she was when one of them had the audacity to comment on her lush figure as she turned.

"What did you say?" she asked, her voice ripe with anger. Is this what the women of this castle had to tolerate? Who the hell did these men think they were?

When they just continued to look down their noses at her she stepped right up to the bigger of the two. "I asked you a question."

"Like I would ever feel the need to answer a common tramp," he sneered feeling confident in his bigger presence. "Dirty shifter," he sneered and she realised that he thought she was a shifter because of how she dressed. Yet another thing she hadn't thought to discuss with her brother. Exactly how was a queen to dress?

Then she shook her head and let the anger consume her. It shouldn't matter what manner of clothes a person wore, what ability they possessed. Everyone should be treated with common decency and she would damn sure make that a priority from this moment on.

She turned back to him and let her hand slide up his thigh, let her body lean into him just a little, just enough to block the other guard's view. "I can be dirty," Aurora whispered. "I can be the dirtiest little girl you've ever seen."

"I bet you can," he replied in a voice laced with the heat of his lust. She could smell it on his skin like a foul odour. He repulsed her and soon he would know not to ever address her again.

Her hand made it to his hip. He leant down his face mere inches from her, his rancid breath bathing her skin. She let both hands lace behind his neck tugging him that extra inch closer and let her anger flow.

Her forehead connected with his nose and the blood gushed as it broke but even before the hit was made her knee was up in his groin planting his balls somewhere up inside his abdominal cavity. At the moment she didn't care where. His scream rent the air, a high piercing echo that sounded indisputably feminine. Her hand jerked the short sword from his belt as he fell to writhe at their feet in a foetal position.

She faced the other guard, her hand comfortable on the grip of the blade. He was angry and not filled with the lust of his comrade. "Come," she motioned and like a bellowing animal he charged. All rage and no grace while she was just the opposite. Never let your opponent make you angry. It gave them the advantage and now that was hers.

She let his momentum take him by her and with a foot to his backside sent him head first into the wall. He hit with a bellow and turned to come at her again when a figure appeared out of nowhere. The man hit the wall with such force that he was nearly unconscious when he dropped. Unfortunately for him that oblivion didn't come.

She watched as Domi knelt before the man, his panther showing in his teeth and eyes as he growled at the man who had dared to come at her with a weapon. "Never are you to even breathe around my mate again. To do so is to die." It was more than a threat and they all knew it. It was a promise.

Nado, Lynx and Micah entered the hall behind them and joined her where she stood. Domi stood and moved from the downed man to join them.

"It is a good thing that I do not need my mates," she turned to face all three men, "or my bodyguard to ensure my safety." They all glared at her and she laughed. She wasn't surprised when her sister joined her.

"Perhaps if the women of the shifter race did not sneak about they would not need protection," Micah said but she had a feeling that his words were meant for her sister who glared at him.

"But I am not a shifter," Aurora said.

"Did you not grow and thrive while among them?" Micah queried. At her silent nod he smiled softly to her. "Then you are one of them, no matter the path that your birth leads you on."

He was right and somehow that knowledge comforted her. She had a feeling that everything was about to spiral out of control. She only hoped that when all the pieces where put together Aslan would still be on her side.

As if conjured from her thoughts the door opened behind her and both Aslan and Wilhelm stepped from the room.

"What the hell happened out here?" Wilhelm bellowed and Aurora realised that they were Wilhelm's men and not her brother's. Those men would have to be weeded out and dealt with, and soon.

Wilhelm marched over to the one that still keened on the floor and kicked him hard enough to break a rib. With a sharp gasp he did his best to quiet but it cost him considerably.

"What did you do to them?" he turned his wrath on their little group but she had little doubt that it was mostly towards the men. Until he turned his eyes directly on Aurora and she felt the heat of his hatred. What was it about her that made him feel such vehemence towards her?

Her mates took position on either side of her but she put a hand to each of their chests before they could speak. She would handle this. It was time to begin opening her brother's eyes to what this man was capable of, to who he really was.

"I was coming to speak to my brother about today's agenda when I was stopped by these two," she began but of course Wilhelm interrupted.

"They are part of my personal guard and know that when the king and I are in private conversations that we are not to be disturbed." It was a sneer and meant to make her feel unwanted. She wanted to laugh, especially when her brother spoke.

"Did you not think to inform them that my sister and their queen has returned to us?" Aslan was angry and it came through loud and clear in his voice. "She is part of the council, a most important part, and is to be included in everything that we discuss."

Wilhelm swallowed several times and Aurora had to bite back a triumphant grin. Whatever hold Wilhelm felt he had on Aslan was not as strong as the man had thought. It appeared that perhaps blood was more important.

Wilhelm nodded with dignity and with a sharp order both men climbed laboriously to their feet. "As you wish my king," he said and took off with both men struggling to follow behind him.

"Shit," Aslan muttered under his breath but Aurora heard it anyway. "Come on in," he motioned to them and shut the door behind them. It was only then that she noticed how the only sound she could hear was that which was within the room. The room must be sound proof somehow which meant her brother had no idea what had taken place outside. Great.

"What has you so upset?" she asked as she walked to him. He seemed to take comfort in the fact that she came to him, to stand beside him.

"I've angered Wilhelm," he sighed. "It was not my intention to make him feel unimportant."

Now it was she who sighed. "I need to ask you something Aslan, something so important that it will decide the course of what is to come."

He looked at her then at the faces of the others in the room. "I know that Uncle Wilhelm can be hard to take at times. He is set in his ways and is quick to judge some. But he has the best in mind, the best for our people."

"The best for our people," Aurora asked letting her voice emphasis the 'our'. "Or what is best for all the people who live here? We are many and we are diverse. None should stand above or below."

Aslan looked confused. "I agree and I am sure that Wilhelm does as well."

"There you would be wrong," Lynx interjected.

"Are you not speaking out of anger since it was one of his men who accidentally stabbed you?" Aslan asked but there was no accusation in his voice.

"Absolutely not considering I thought it was one of yours until you just cleared that up for me," Lynx stated and met Aurora's gaze. "But that would explain some things."

"It would appear that perhaps we are all targets," Micah said and let his eyes lock with Aslan's. "And you most of all, especially now."

"What are you talking about?" Aslan asked at the same time that Aurora asked a question.

"Why would you think he was in more danger now?" she asked Micah. "There are more of us here to watch, more of us that know what is actually happening."

"And it is just for that reason that we must all have a plan in place before we leave this room," Micah stated with calm. "There are plenty of outsiders now that could be blamed for any number of things," his gaze went back to Aslan. "Including an assassination."

"Assassination?" asked Aslan. "Just what the hell are you all talking about?"

"Perhaps you should have a seat," Aurora said and pointed to the chairs they had sat in. "And a drink. This won't be a pretty conversation. You are going to hear things that you won't want to believe but all of our lives just might depend on whether you do or not."

"I'm still not following," Aslan said but he sat in the chair, his gaze on Aurora. She realised that it was the fact that she was his sister that just might convince him to take a chance on her, on them.

"It is about Wilhelm," she said coming over to sit beside him. "He is not who you think, not who he wants you to believe he is."

"And if we don't work together," Micah added, "he will do everything in his power to kill us all." He stopped in front of them and looked down at Aslan. "And with both the king and queen out of the way, rule will fall to him, with no one left to stand in his way."

"That is nonsense," Aslan stated shaking his head. "If he wanted me dead he could have killed me years ago, when I was small and helpless."

It was Domi who spoke now. "With your mother recently assassinated and your sister missing just how helpless do you believe you were?"

"He would have had to let you live," Nado added. "You were the last of the royal family and the people would have all been watching you."

Aslan seemed to be thinking of things and Aurora almost regretted her next question.

"How many people close to you have died within the last few years?" she asked him and wasn't surprised when she saw the first touch of confusion in his eyes.

"The woman who took care of me," he said, "she died when I was a teenager. I was away with Wilhelm and she was coming to visit me. Her letter said that there were secrets she could no longer keep from me." He looked up at her, at all of them, and seemed so sad. "She never reached me."

"Anyone else?" It was hard for Aurora to watch her brother learn just what Wilhelm had managed to do to control him.

"Goddess," he groaned. "Over the last ten years it seems that everyone close to me has died or disappeared. I never thought," he stopped and swallowed several times. "Are you certain that any of this is not just coincidence?"

"For your sake I wish that it was," Aurora said and leaned over to take his hand in hers. "But there is just too much that doesn't add up."

"What else?" Aslan asked and it was as if he aged right before their eyes.

"I was sent here for two purposes," Micah said. "Six months ago an emissary of my people was sent to your shores with orders to speak directly to you. We had heard murmurs of a plot to kill you."

"Murmurs?" Aslan muttered. "I hear those every day. Most amount to nothing more than misinterpretation."

"My people have ways of sorting truth from lies," Micah said. "And we found this one to be important enough to send someone to warn you."

"No one ever reached me," Aslan said.

"No, he didn't," Micah agreed and for the first time his eyes glowed with sharp anger. "He was captured when he reached your shores and even now is tortured within your walls."

Aslan came to his feet. "That is a hell of an accusation to make."

"But one he can back up," Lynx put in. "I've seen his brother. I've been to the rooms below the castle. I've smelled the horrors that have taken place below."

"What rooms? What are you talking about?" Aslan seemed lost, and broken, and the horror on his face brought tears to Aurora's eyes. No matter where the fault lay, Aslan would carry the blame on his shoulders. He would feel it as his failure and would punish himself as he saw fit.

"I can show you," Lynx said. "When we have decided what to do, when we know what steps we should take."

"I didn't know," Aslan muttered. "What kind of king has no idea of the evil within his own home? Within his own family?" His gaze took them all in and there was a small bit of pleading when he looked at Aurora again. "Are you sure that the blame for all of this lies with Wilhelm? Could it not be someone else just trying to make it appear as if he is to blame?"

"I don't believe so," Aurora answered honestly and after holding her gaze for a moment her brother nodded and turned away.

"I have failed the people then," he said. "I will remove myself as king. When I introduce you officially today it will be done."

"Are you crazy?" Aurora yelled. "Or just selfish?"

"What?" Aslan turned back to stare at her.

"Your people need you more than ever now," Aurora stated. "And you are just going to walk away? I don't think so." She stormed over to where he stood and gave him a solid thump on his chest. "You will hear more negatives before all is said and done. You will have to hear it and push it aside for now. I am back and for the first time since our mother's death we will stand together as one. We will do what she would have expected us to do. We will do what is best for the people."

He nodded once and pulled her close into his embrace. She figured he would be safe from her mates as he was her brother, but she wasn't surprised when the rumble of a cat filled the room. Domi would have to work on that.

"You have the advantage," she told her brother. "You know Wilhelm better than any of us."

"Or not as well, it would seem," he muttered.

"We will work together and find the truth," she vowed. "And once it is known we will deal with it together."

"Yes," he agreed and she stepped back from him. He seemed to know that she was holding something back. "What more are you not telling me?"

She sighed and let her gaze move to her mates, her sister. "I have a request to make and it will have to be agreed on by us all." She took a deep breath and just plunged in. "I'd like to bring my mother, Lydia, here."

Aslan tensed beside her and Lynx's bellow of "NO" filled the room.

"She knows what we couldn't possibly know," Aurora argued. "She has answers, facts that we need to know."

"She is right," Nado said and both Domi and Micah agreed.

"We will watch over and protect her," Aurora said as she walked over to take her sister's hands. "Nothing will happen to her."

Lynx's eyes were filled with tears but her strength was too strong to allow her to shed them. Instead she just nodded and Aurora knew that it cost her sister to agree. Aurora was worried as well. If Wilhelm meant to kill them all what might he do to someone who actually was there when all this began?

Aurora held her sister's hand and turned so that she faced all four men in the room. "I don't believe my mother, our mother," she said to Aslan, "died as is said. I think there is more to the story. And I believe that Wilhelm plays a big part in that." She let her eyes plead with Aslan. "Do we not owe it to her to try to discover the truth? The real truth of what happened that day?"

Something tugged at Aslan's mind, like a memory that was trying to surface but had to wade through too much to get there. He thought he heard a soft voice whisper that when the time was right he would know. But no one in the room had spoken that he was aware of. He nodded and he could see the relief on his sister's face.

"Lydia will be welcome here," he said. "I will have some of my most trusted keep their eyes and ears on Wilhelm and his men."

"I pray that will be enough," Lynx said and Aslan felt her worry as his own. Sometimes it felt as if this sister of his twin was his relative as well. Perhaps it was the fact that she was Aurora's little sister. It made him think of her as his little sister as well. Part of him felt as if his whole world was tumbling down, crumbling to ashes. His life seemed to be built on betrayal and lies. And yet here in this room he finally had the only family that ever really mattered to him. As a king he felt that he had failed so far, as a brother he vowed that he never would.

He moved over to a panel beside the fireplace and moved it aside to reveal a room that he thought even Wilhelm didn't know about. He motioned everyone in and saw the different expressions on their faces as they took in the long table and the different weapons that graced the walls.

He felt his first real smile of the day tug his lips. "I may be king but I am still a warrior."

Aurora's face lit up and he almost laughed. His sister was beautiful, a natural with weapons. He promised himself that he would ensure that nothing ever happened to her while he was alive.

He slid the panel back closed and pointed to the table. "Let's have a seat and plan."

"Let's plan quickly," Aurora said as she came to the table beside him. "Action is needed before this hour ends."

Everyone took a chair and it felt right when he sat with Aurora on his right. She was his right hand. No one would take her from him again.

Wilhelm growled as silence met his ears now. Where the hell had they moved to? He had set this room so that he would be able to hear everything that was said in the King's office. Everything had been going as planned until Aurora had arrived. If his men had done their jobs right then she would be dead by now. Instead he was down four men. The two that her shifter family had killed and the two that he had just disposed of. If a woman could best them then what use were they to him? Whether she was queen or not should mean little.

He looked up when his most trusted warrior entered the room. "I have another task for you," he said. "Make sure you do not fail me. They intend to bring the shifter girl's mother to the castle, to interrogate her." He let his gaze meet his warrior's. "It is my wish that she never reach the castle."

With a nod the warrior left. Wilhelm did not feel a need to worry but he did feel a need to disappear for a while. He had no idea how long he had before they came down to where his dungeons were. Not enough time to do the things he needed but perhaps enough to do some. He turned to the other two men who were in the room with him.

"Move those that you can," he ordered. "But when you feel that there is no more time start killing them. It is important that you leave no prisoners alive."

"Yes sir," they both nodded and turned to do his bidding, weapons already being placed in their hands.

He would have to disappear for a bit. Luckily he had just the place to go, a place close enough that he would still know everything that happened here. And when the time was right he would kill everyone who stood in his way. Starting with that little bitch Aurora.

Chapter Nine

In less than an hour they were making their way through the halls to the kitchen where Lynx swore a secret door was. Aurora prayed that they were not too late. Things seemed way to quiet and it made her wonder if Wilhelm hadn't figured out their plans while they were making them. Somehow it wouldn't surprise her.

They had spent precious minutes divining the best course of action and waiting for Aslan's most trusted warriors to arrive. But as soon as they entered the room she caught her first glimpse of the boy her brother must have been at one time in the camaraderie he shared with them.

First to arrive were Piers and Seer. It was easy to see that they were the best of friends and she hadn't been surprised to find out that they were cousins. There was an ease and comfort to them that bespoke of knowing each other very well. They were both tall with brown wavy hair and big green eyes, though Piers' were darker. They were quick to greet Aslan with a warm embrace. And Aslan was quick to smile and return their hug of friendship.

Next were Lake and Lincoln, both golden haired charmers. Lake had the softest blue eyes she had ever seen while Lincoln's were nearly black. The same laughs and hugs were exchanged and for the first time Aurora wondered what it would have been like to grow to womanhood with her brother at her side. But fate hadn't given them that and so they came together now. At least now she had hope that her brother's youth had at least been filled with friendship and laughter as well, and maybe a bit of mischief every now and then.

Aslan had been so proud to introduce her to those men he so obviously held near and dear. From the looks the bond was especially tight between Aslan, Piers and Seer. They all greeted her by going to bended knee, bowing their heads and placing right fist to heart. It was the same thing she had received from the warriors in the glen when she had pulled the sword. She understood that it was their way of swearing fealty to their newly discovered queen. She had to admit she got a certain thrill out of men falling to their knees in front of her.

Greetings and introductions out of the way and they had filled the warriors in on their discoveries and plans. It was easy to read the heartbreak in Aslan's eyes, to see that even now he prayed for other answers. But his friends didn't seem to share his doubt and she was curious just how much they had kept from him out of misguided loyalty. She might find out once this was all over. But first they had a Danuja to save, and maybe a few others as well.

All bowed when she entered and seemed awed that her brother walked behind her. But she had never been one to take a backseat to others and she wouldn't start now. It was good enough in her opinion that she stayed behind her mates and Lynx. Yet she had little doubt that once Lynx showed them where the door was she would be shuffled to the back as well.

As Lynx moved around the kitchen grew deathly quiet. It seemed they all knew what they were searching for but perhaps fear kept them from helping. Aurora hoped they found the door soon.

It was a young girl who stepped forward, shy and obviously nervous. Lynx glanced at the girl and smiled. Then she shifted into a small tabby cat that the girl seemed to recognise.

"It was you who went down the stairs with me," the girl exclaimed and picked Lynx up and gave her a quick squeeze. Suddenly the girl squeaked and dropped Lynx back to the floor. "I'm so sorry. I didn't mean to harm you."

"No harm done," Nado reassured the girl. "Shifters are a resilient lot."

"You are the one who delivers the tray to the prisoner below," Micah said as he stepped forward.

The girl gasped and backed up. "How did you escape him?"

Micah's feral expression softened at the girl's fear. "I am not he but I seek him, and quickly before it is too late."

"You know where the door is?" Aslan stepped forward now and claimed her attention. It would have been funny the way the girl's head bobbled around on her neck as she turned to each new person. But the circumstances were far too serious to see the humour just yet. Time was running out. Aurora could feel it and she sensed the others could as well.

The girl nodded and crossed the kitchen by the stove. She pulled a cabinet open and with a press of her fingers a panel slid open inside. A staircase was revealed that descended into the depths of the castle. Lynx, who had maintained her tabby form, shot through the opening and disappeared into the darkness beyond. With a roar Domi leapt and changed to panther mid air hitting the stairs on all fours and taking off after Aurora's sister.

Nado glanced at her and smiled before doing the same. She could feel the tension in Micah and knew that he wanted to sprint after them as well. But honestly she didn't know which prompted him more. His need to find his brother or his need to get to her sister. There was something brewing there and she wished her sister the best. Micah seemed a wise and good man. She could ask no more for her sister.

"What are we waiting for?" she asked the men still in the kitchen with her. "Let's see where these stairs lead." With a nod to her brother she drew her sword and took off down the dark stairs towards the glow of light at the bottom. Now was when they finally found out just what Wilhelm had hidden down here.

The stench hit their noses before they even made it to the bottom of the stairs. Vomit, sweat and blood. It was quite a combination and Aurora found herself gagging a little. What atrocities had been practiced down here?

Reaching the bottom of the stairs they followed the corridor, sensing that her mates, sister and Micah had gone one way at the split in the hallway, Aurora led those with her in the other. And anger grew. Doors were opened in the stone wall but all that greeted them were empty rooms or worse. Bodies that they had been too late to save. The stench was overpowering in some rooms, rooms where perhaps the torture had been greatest.

At the end of the corridor a man was chained to the wall. At their approach his eyes lifted though it was impossible for him to lift his head. He was pure skin and bones and Aurora was enraged at his appearance. But it was nothing compared to Aslan's and it didn't take her long to realise two things. Micah, Piers and Seer hadn't followed her and her brother and his remaining friends knew this man.

"You are dead," Aslan bellowed as he checked the chains searching no doubt for the easiest way to free the man. "I was told you were dead."

"Only a matter of time," the old man rasped in a voice so weak it was barely above a whisper.

"How could this have happened?" Aslan raged.

"Wilhelm," was the response and what little bit of hope and doubt of Wilhelm's guilt that remained in her brother disappeared. It was as if a veil descended along Aslan's face. Suddenly before her was the warrior, the man of power and knowing what had brought the change made her sad.

"He will die for what he has done," Aslan promised the man and leaning in he placed his head next to the man's. "I knew not of this Marcus. By all I am I swear to you that I knew not."

"You were well protected," was the soft reply. "I did my best and now it will be up to my sons."

Aslan turned and seemed to realise that not everyone who came down the stairs was with him. "Find them," he commanded and Lake took off at a run back down the corridor.

"Hold still and let me try something," Aurora said and with a mighty swing of her sword she managed to sever the top of the chains that held Marcus to the wall. It had been her hope that the magic in her sword would sever whatever magic held the chains to the wall. And it had.

Aslan cradled Marcus as he fell, slowly lowering him instead. The man looked up for the first time and saw Aurora.

"Ona," he breathed and his eyes grew wide. She shook her head and a bit of the sudden light that had filled as his eyes dimmed. "I will see her soon enough."

"This is Aurora," Aslan told him. "She has finally come home."

A nod and a smile now. "I'm glad that I lived long enough to see the two of you reunited. At least I will die with peace."

A yell and the crash of running feet behind them and Piers and Seer joined Aslan on the floor by Marcus. Seer took the man in his arms and it was heart wrenching to see the tears on his face.

Piers clasped one of his hands and leaned in, his head resting atop his father's. "You live. 'Tis the greatest of all miracles."

"Only but a moment longer my son," Marcus whispered. "Only long enough to gaze upon those I love once more. The goddess in generous to an old soul."

"How could he have faked your death so well?" Aslan demanded. "How could we have not known that you were alive?"

"His power is greater than you realise," Marcus said. "There is a dark magic to him that cannot be overlooked."

"I will find him and give him the same fate that he has given to you," Piers vowed, cradling Marcus' hand.

"As will I," Seer swore.

"And I," Aslan stated.

When the old man looked to Aurora she shook her head. "With a dark magic, this is not the fate meant for one such as him." She motioned to the gloom around them, to the wall where Marcus had so recently hung. "He would only feed on this. I shall promise you a slow death for him, one filled with pain greater than he has ever known. I promise you that his blood will pay for all he has wrought."

"You are your mother's daughter," he smiled softly. She could see the light fading from him and knew that the end was near for him. "And perhaps you have a bit of your uncle in you as well."

His eyes closed and a smile graced his face. They all watched as he drew his last breath. Silence filled the corridor. She could feel the grief and anger that poured off of the men around her.

Piers was the first to stand. He turned to Aurora and held his hand out to her. She took it in both of hers and squeezed it tight. He slowly pulled it from her and walked away. Seer was next. The same thing. It was so different seeing them walk out of the corridor. Gone was the swagger of a soldier ready for battle. Now it was men weighed down with sorrow.

Aslan was the last to rise, the last to turn and take her hand. "We will avenge our blood," he swore.

"So you think Wilhelm had something to do with our mother's death?" Aurora asked.

Aslan shook his head. "I honestly don't know. It wouldn't surprise me at this point."

"Then what are you talking about?" Aurora ask with confusion.

"Marcus," he swallowed and hung his head for a minute. "Our uncle, the king."

"What?" Aurora was even more confused now. "You're king."

"As Queen Ona's son the title passed to me when Marcus was presumed dead. Just as the sword goes to you. When I die the title of king will pass to your first born son as with your death the sword will pass to your first born daughter. That is how it is with our people. The line passes from daughter to daughter."

"Our uncle?" she took another look at the man before her and now understood why he had thought she was Ona, her mother. What was Wilhelm after? Did he want the throne for his own? And if that was the way things passed down then why would he even think that he had a chance? He was her father's brother and thus his only link to the throne was through his brother's marriage to her mother. This made less and less sense the more she found out.

But there was no time to contemplate those questions now. There was a roar from the other end of the corridor, from the corridor they had not chosen. And it was time she and her brother joined the others. Time to see if they were at least in time to save Merced.

The roar sounded again and this time she recognised it. The lion had always been one of her sister's favourite forms and one she used often. That roar was her sister and Lynx did not sound happy. Aurora took off at a run with Aslan, Lake and Lincoln close behind her. She flew around the corner and felt her heart stop.

Nado lay silent and unmoving on the floor. No visible blood to explain why he was down. Micah was nowhere to be seen and Lynx and Domi had two men cornered against a portion of the wall. And there was something in the air, a deeper, darker magic that seemed liked a forcefield before them. What powers did Wilhelm hold at his fingertips?

She ran to Nado first. The smell of magic was strong on him, as if he had been burned by it. He did not move when she touched him but she caught her breath when she found a solid pulse. He was alive and for now that was all that mattered. She had to know what had happened to him. With a great warrior's cry she flew towards the two men cornered.

The men seemed to shake harder at her presence which would have been funny at any other time. They were already cornered by a panther and a lion, what about her could be scarier than that? It was laughable, but no one was laughing. She never slowed down, processed it all as she ran. Then with a leap and a swing of her sword one was dead. Her sword clanged against the wall as she cleaved through skin and bone severing his head from his body.

The other man took up a high keening wail that echoed around them. He dropped his weapon and dropped to his knees begging for his life. Domi and Lynx backed up and transformed back to their human skins while Aslan stepped forward to her.

"We need these men to find out all we can about this," he motioned to the space around them.

"It only takes one to talk," she replied before taking her blade and laying it aside the neck of the man kneeled before her. "And I pray the answers you have are the right ones. For your sake."

"Yes! Yes! Yes!" the man screamed, sobbing and managing to look quite pathetic. These were the men Wilhelm sought out? What a waste of life.

She turned from him, leaving him to Aslan and the other warriors for the moment. "What happened here?" she demanded of Lynx and Domi.

Domi was beside Nado and she knew that her mate was just as upset as she was at the sight of Nado so still. A look passed between them and it was filled with anxiety, worry and love on both their parts. But it was Lynx who replied.

"There is some type of force field here," and she indicated what looked to Aurora like just more wall obscured by darkness.

"The wall?" Aurora asked.

"No, and yet made to appear as such," Lynx stated. "Micah was able to pass through and once I was able to as well," she swallowed hard and when she looked up it was with tears in her eyes. "Which is why I told Nado to follow Micah. I thought he would be able to get through as well. But when I passed through it was as a tabby and I was in the arms of a Danuja."

"Merced," Aurora stated and Lynx nodded. "So we have found him and now lost Micah as well?"

"Micah was able to pass through but cannot get back to us. His magic isn't that strong. He is a healer, sort of like a holy man for his people. Merced would be able to but he is too weak. Micah has gone into some kind of a trance to try and heal Merced. We haven't heard from him in a while and I am worried for them both." Aurora could hear the tears in Lynx's voice and she realised that her sister was developing feelings for these two Danuja men. She prayed they could get both of the Danuja free of Wilhelm's prison.

"You," she turned back to the remaining man, a guard for Wilhelm most likely. "Tell me what you know of this magic. Now. And it had best be useful."

"'Tis Danuja magic," the man stammered. "Placed by one to contain one."

"And?" Aurora said, making a point to lift her sword, the blade still stained red.

He swallowed hard. "There is some type of box set high at the top that holds the cell in place. Only by removing it will it cease."

"If I have to prompt you one more time you will lose a limb," Aurora promised. "You do not need those to answer questions."

"At the top," he squealed pointing his finger up high to the ceiling just above the wall. "You can't see the box but you can see where the wall appears just a bit darker in one spot. That is what you are aiming for."

Aurora glanced at the spot and saw what he was talking about. It was too high for her to reach with her sword and she had no other weapon at her disposal. Her frustration was growing. It was Piers who stepped forward removing a small dagger with a wicked curve from his belt. Taking careful aim he threw it with speed and complete accuracy.

There was a crackle and a pop and the wall disappeared revealing the prone shapes of two huge men. Micah and Merced. Lynx yelled and ran to them while Aurora went back to where her mates were. Nado seemed to be coming around now and she wanted to be there when his eyes opened. She took Domi's hand in hers and let Lynx and the others take care of the rest. For the moment she was just a woman who needed to be sure her mate was all right.

Lynx hurried to the two men. Micah was weak, his pulse so soft it took her twice to find it. Merced did not appear to be breathing at all. Without thought she tilted his head back, opened his mouth and pinched his nose. Leaning in she sealed her mouth to his and exhaled, blowing her breath into him. Three times she did this before he gasped and finally breathed on his own.

His beautiful golden eyes with flecks of brown opened slowly to greet her. Sensing that he would be fine she turned to Micah which was easy since she knelt between them.

"Micah," she said softly. "Wake up. We still have things to talk about remember?" She would discuss whatever he wanted, her wandering ways or anything, if only he would open his eyes.

"You give me breath," Merced sounded awed by this as he sat up beside her.

"Yes," she nodded still focused on Micah. "But your brother is still weak. Is there anything you can do to help him?"

Merced stared at her for a moment before turning to his brother. He inhaled deeply and leaned into his brother's face before exhaling. She watched in amazement as a golden glow seemed to leave his mouth and sink into Micah's skin. Within mere seconds Micah was opening his eyes and sitting up beside her. Without thought Lynx launched herself at him raining kisses over his face.

"Micah," she smiled. "I thought I had lost you."

"Not so easily little cat," he whispered.

"You should not be so foolish brother," Merced interrupted them and Lynx would swear that she heard anger in his voice. "You almost lost your life and yet still it would not have saved me."

"And yet here you are?" Micah stated.

"No thanks to you," Merced replied. "It was your little cat that breathed life into me."

Micah gasped and looked down at Lynx. "She breathed into you?" he asked and she was getting confused.

"Yes," Merced said and she could almost feel Micah deflating like a balloon. It must have shown on his face as well for Merced's voice softened with his next words.

"She did not know," Merced said and placed his hand on Micah's shoulder to give it a squeeze.

"It matters not," Micah said and easing her from his lap he stood. "The law is clear. What is to be is to be."

"Micah," Merced helped Lynx to her feet as Micah stood.

"Good to have you back brother," was all that Micah said as he turned to the rest of the group, leaving Lynx standing with Merced.

"What just happened here?" she asked quietly looking up at the big man.

"It seems that you and I will be having a talk little cat," Merced said. "But first there are other things to see to."

She stood alone for a moment watching the ones around her. The joy on her sister's face as Nado sat up and embraced Aurora. The way Domi's face tilted into a half grin as Nado said something. The stance of the warriors that surrounded them and the look of pleasure on Aslan's face as he took in his sister's happiness. Then she focused on her Danuja. Brothers reunited and yet there seemed such distance between them. What had just happened? She knew that it had something to do with her and breathing into Merced. She wondered how long she would have to wait before finding out.

Lynx was never one to back down from anything. She knew that her fear for them meant that she cared for them more than just a friend. There was something between them, all three of them and she was bound and determined to find out exactly what it was. And explore it to the fullest. She was also sure that Micah and Merced felt something for her as well. She wasn't sure what Danuja culture allowed though. That would be something she planned to find out about as soon as time presented itself. One thing was sure. She was not letting either of them walk out of her life without a fight.

"Come," Aslan said. "We have much left to do before the ceremony later."

"The prisoner?" Seer asked.

It was Aurora who answered. "One by one I want him to carry the bodies of those still here out to the courtyard. Let the people see what he has done, what Wilhelm has wrought within these very walls. When the last body is brought forth, he is to be chained to the outside wall."

"No, please I beg of you," the guard implored.

"I wonder how many times you heard those very words and ignored them," she murmured. "You made your choice when you decided to go against your king and work for Wilhelm."

"But I did not know that it was against the king," the man tried to say and Aurora was in his face instantly.

"Don't insult me with your lies," she threatened. "I've only met him recently and even I can tell that this hell is nothing that would ever be sanctioned by Aslan."

He cowered before her. "You will carry everybody out of here and place them so that if there is family still here they can be claimed and buried as is just and right. And when all that remains are those that no one knows or recognises you will personally dig every grave. Then you will be put to the wall." She turned to Lake and Lincoln. "Take him now and see that he carries every one of my orders out."

Both men placed right fist to their hearts and bowed their heads. "Yes, my Queen."

"Wilhelm will hear of this and when you put him on the wall he will have him killed," Aslan stated once the man was gone.

"Yes," Aurora agreed.

Aslan looked at her. "You know this and still that is your plan?"

"There is no mercy in me for a man who chose to torture others," she said. "And it will be good for the people to see what we do to traitors and how Wilhelm has no care to save what he uses. And just maybe when this man who willingly chose to do evil dies he will have repented and begged the goddess for forgiveness because it is not mine to give."

"You are the queen that our people need," Aslan stated.

"We will see in just a few short hours," Aurora stated. "Word of what I have done here will spread before tonight's ceremony. We will see how the people greet me then."

Chapter Ten

She was nervous, more nervous than she had ever been. In just a few short hours she would stand before the people and be judged as worthy or not. Of her people, of her blood, of her mother. It was a difficult thing to process. She tried to blow it off, to act as if it meant little to her. But her mates could tell that it was eating her up inside.

Nado was still on the bed behind her. He had been knocked out by a powerful jolt of magic when he had attempted to cross the invisible veil with Micah. She could smell the evil of the magic and considered them all damn lucky that her man hadn't died. A shudder raced down her spine once more as she thought of that possibility.

"Relax," his sweet voice surrounded her just as his arms embraced her and pulled her back against him. "I am fine now."

"You should be in bed still, Nado," she breathed closing her eyes and feeling the tears build behind her eyes. So much. Was it all more than they could bear?

She felt Domi join them before he spoke. They were both so much a part of her that she feared if one of them died they all would.

"There is nothing to fear, my love," Domi said coming to stand beside her. "What is meant to be is meant to be. And no amount of worry will change that."

She opened her eyes and for once couldn't stop the tears that escaped. She eased from Nado's embrace and turned so that she could face them both. "And if that fate means that we are to be here? Within these walls?"

"Foolish woman," Nado said and grinned as he reached out to catch one teardrop on his fingertip. "Not even walls can keep us apart."

Domi of course looked furious. He jerked her to him with a snarl. "Do you honestly believe that anything would make us leave your side? Ever?"

"Not willingly," she smiled tenderly. "But how will you ever truly be happy cooped up here with me? Be honest with me. Is this what you would have chosen for us? This could not be what you envisioned when you chose me for mate."

"No," Domi said. "I envisioned lots of sun and water and foreplay and hours, days, of non-stop fucking."

She felt the heat of desire flood her at his carnal words, at the predatory look that he wore so well.

"And we'll still have that," he continued. "On many occasions we will have just that. But we will also have so much more. You are queen, Aurora. And with that comes a power that few will ever know."

"I never wanted it," she tried to tell them. "I never knew it was mine."

"No," Nado agreed. "But it is your destiny just the same. And now it is ours. Where you go, we will as well. When your name is spoken ours will be linked. You are their queen, their hope and salvation. But you are our life, our blood, the very air we breathe. Our journey may not be the one any of us anticipated. But it is still our journey and we will continue it as one."

"You don't regret..." she began but it was Domi who stopped her again.

"Don't even think to say something stupid here," he warned. "You are the most intelligent woman I have ever known and I will accept no less from you now."

"I'm going to take that as a compliment," she said with a level look his way.

"You worry that you are not the queen that your people need," Nado said. "You worry that you will not live up to the legend of the mother you never knew."

The tears came again. Gods, they knew her so well.

"The truth is that you are exactly what they need at exactly the time that they need it," Domi stated quietly. "The power you exerted today, the confidence that surrounds you here is breathtaking."

"You have always been beautiful Aurora," Nado said. "But since we have come here it is like watching you bloom more and more every day so that your sheer beauty overpowers everything else around you."

"You are strength, honour and loyalty," Domi said. "No man who stands at your side needs to ever fear that you will desert him or leave him to face the enemy alone. No woman here will ever fear that they will be spoken down to or abused while you hold reign. No shifter, no native, none with magic inside them need ever fear that you will sneer or look down on them because of the title you hold."

"Already the people speak of you with awe and respect," Nado added. "Both men and women bow to you for those same feelings. You are what they have prayed for."

She could feel the tears drying on her cheeks. It was a lot of knowledge, a lot of responsibility. But she could and would carry it. "I just pray that I do not fail them," she spoke softly. "Or worse, fail you."

"Woman," Domi said with a roar as he picked her up and threw her over his shoulder. His hand came down with a hard smack on her ass. The sting travelled up her spine, over her shoulders, down to her nipples which tightened further and continued its circle to her pussy which flushed wetter with desire. "Perhaps you need a reminder of whose woman you are."

His hand fell on her ass again just before she fell through the air until her back met the bed.

"Yes, maybe I need just that," she breathed and wiggled on the bed.

Domi grinned down at her and it was positively primal. His panther was so dominant in him. And it made her so fucking hot when he rumbled the way he was right now.

"Are you purring Domi?" she asked with a laugh.

"Only for you," he whispered before leaning down so that his breath feathered across her parted lips. "Only ever for you."

He kissed her then and it was so sweet, so perfect. No lust in his touch though it coursed through both their bodies. No this was love in its sheerest and most complete form. In hours she would formally take on the mantle of queen. But for now she was only a woman who needed the comfort of her mates.

"Love me," she whispered as he pulled from her, breaking their kiss.

"Always," he promised slipping back further and reaching for her shoes.

"Forever," Nado said as he joined her on the bed. He was already deliciously naked his cock jutting from his body curving up to his belly button. Damn how she enjoyed that wicked curve.

He reached for her shirt while Domi finished with her boots and worked on her pants until she was finally naked as well. She pounced on Nado while Domi stripped beside the bed. On her hands and knees she loomed over him reaching down to take his cock in her hand giving it a squeeze before slowly gliding her fingers down his shaft. Her mouth watered and the tip of his cock gleamed with a tiny drop that she couldn't deny herself.

She bent her head and slid her tongue over the head of his cock loving the taste that filled her mouth. One tiny drip of fluid and she was so greedy for more. She took the entire head into her mouth and sucked hard working her tongue at the notch just under the head. Her fingers squeezed and stroked coming up to meet her mouth before heading back down. She could feel his balls swelling with more cum and she wanted to suck every drop of it from him.

With a cry Nado's cock slipped free of her mouth and her fingers clenched tighter around him drawing a moan from him as well. Domi had gone to his knees beside the bed so that his face was level with her cunt as he reached for her. His grip tightened on her hips as he plunged his tongue deeper into her pussy. The man could fuck with anything, cock, mouth or fingers. He stole her breath and kept her from feeding her other hunger. She took Nado again sucking harder and using her teeth to nip while tonguing every inch she could.

"Fuck," Nado said as he arched into her, one hand reaching out to stoke her hair.

"We'll get to that very soon," Domi said in between tongue fucking her pussy. One finger came up to circle her clit and he pinched the blossoming bud between that finger and thumb.

She cried out again and felt her first orgasm rip through her. Nado's cock slipped free again as Domi kept his tongue and fingers working pushing her into yet another orgasm. She shook, barely managing to stay on her knees when he finally quit his assault on her spasming pussy.

"Now we get to the fucking," Domi said and she could hear the arrogance in his voice. But honestly he deserved to feel arrogant. The man was amazing. Nado was the only one who could hold his own against Domi. And thank the goddess she never had to choose between them. No, she was the lucky girl that got to have them both.

Nado slid from under her and she heard him rustling in a bag. A tube appeared on the bed and she recognised it from before as the oil of love that the shifters used for anal sex. She was in for a hell of a fucking from her mates and she was more than ready for it.

"Which?" Nado asked Domi and she wanted to scream with frustration. She wanted those thick cocks buried deep inside her right now.

Domi stood beside the bed, one hand on the arch of her back as the other took the tube from the bed. She heard him snap it open and pour some into his palm before she felt it drip between the cheeks of her ass. She honestly didn't care which of them it was as long as they entered her soon.

"Hurry," she breathed then cried out as Domi did just that. He had the tip of his well oiled dick at her back entrance before the word fully left her mouth and with one slow easy thrust he filled her with his wide cock. The burn as he entered. The painful pleasure as he pushed through the first tight ring of muscle. The ache when he was fully seated and unmoving.

"Fuck me," she cried trying to move her hips to do just that. But he held her still, held them tightly together.

"You better get inside that snug little pussy soon or I'm going to come," Domi said and his voice was laced with the control he was using to keep from doing just that.

"Fuck," Nado said and she would have laughed if she had the breath left inside her. Watching him manoeuvre and shift on the bed until he could slide beneath her his legs going between hers and Domi's until his feet must have hit the floor. His cock was aligned perfectly with her wet pussy and she helped him by reaching down to line him up with her opening. He eased the tip in before stopping and looking up at her.

"You better hold on tight," he warned her and waited until she moved her hands so that they gripped his shoulders. It was a good thing that he had.

He thrust hard and deep and she felt like she would split wide open. A cry left her again as they both moved in tandem. Both cocks filling her at the same time at a fast and furious pace. She screamed, arched and bucked between them. It was incredible. She felt wild and bent lower to clamp her teeth onto Nado's chest. His cry joined hers and amazingly it seemed as if they fucked her harder, faster until she honestly felt like the pleasure exploding throughout her body just might make her explode as well.

"I'm going to fucking explode inside your tight little ass," Domi yelled out and moving one hand he reached between her and Nado and found her clit giving it a hard squeeze that had her coming with him.

With a shout of his own Nado joined them. She could feel the fiery heat of their releases filling her, soaking into her very skin it seemed and she spiralled just a bit higher in her own release. She loved them, loved their ease with each other as well as her. Domi had no reserve about touching her when he might be touching Nado as well and the same was true of Nado. The truth was that to her mates it was all about ensuring her pleasure and that made her realise once more just how lucky she was.

"I love you," she whispered as she collapsed against Nado's chest. She felt Domi slide his hand up between her and Nado until he could cup her breast.

"I love you," Nado breathed and a kiss whispered across the top of her head. Domi's hand shifted between her breasts so that he seemed to be cupping her heartbeat itself.

"You are the very beat of my heart," Domi said. "My reason for being."

She could feel the tears burning her eyes once more.

"Well, if you want to get all dramatic about it," Nado said and she could feel the humour in his chest.

She laughed and couldn't seem to stop. Nado joined her and soon she heard Domi's snort turn into full blown laughter as well. It was such a freeing moment, exactly the one that they needed. Life would not be easy for them. There would be struggle and battle and perhaps even death in their future. And as they seemed to think that her people would depend on her, she would depend on her mates. They often knew what she needed before she did. That would be important in the days and weeks to come.

In a few hours she would officially be queen. But for right now she could simply be a woman in love.

It was surreal as she stood there in the total silence that followed her brother's introduction of her. Aurora. Queen Ona's daughter and rightful queen. She had chosen to wear the clothes she was use to, those of the shifter. She could fight in the leathers. They were comfortable and kept her grounded in who she was, a reminder that she was more than a title.

She faced the crowd, and it was a huge crowd, with bated breath, not yet sure of just what she would say, only hoping that the words would come to her as she needed them. She recognised Piers, Seer, Lincoln and Lake where they stood at the front of the large number of warriors present. Micah and Merced stood to the side and there seemed to be something wrong between them, which was strange since they were only hours reunited.

Lynx stood to the side with Aurora's mates. She wanted to laugh as she took them in. All three held the same pose with legs shoulder width apart and arms crossed over their chests. Lynx stood between them and it gave Aurora a glimpse of what she must look like when she stood between her mates.

Her brother stood to her left and a little behind her. They were all around her but for the moment she had never felt more alone.

"Mother give me courage and wisdom," she whispered. It was now or never.

"I did not come to you seeking this. I never knew that this was my destiny," she began and her voice luckily rang out loud and strong, not betraying the nerves that still coursed through her. "I never knew that my mother was queen though I know many stories of my mother the woman. I never knew that I had a twin brother or that he was looking for me. I did not leave you and I did not choose to stay from you. But I do now choose to stand with you. I came here not by chance or circumstance but through the actions of one that so many of you have come to trust." She could feel the tension in Aslan and wanted to turn to him but didn't. "I know not what the future may hold for us. I cannot promise you forever any more than my mother could. But I can promise you that I will fight for justice and for truth. As many of you know, today we discovered evidence that many atrocities occurred right here on our home ground. People were tortured and murdered on the whim of one man. As of today Wilhelm Mulvane is considered an enemy of the state as well as any man or woman who chooses to walk by his side. We know not how deep his betrayal burrows in our midst. But we will find out. We will not stop until he is brought to justice." There was a smattering of applause as well as numerous murmurs that went through the crowd. She took a deep breath before winding down. "I stand before you a warrior who grew and thrived among shifters, a woman mated to two panthers. I do not judge and I will not tolerate such behaviour from others. We are all special and gifted with our individual forms of magic. And only together will we find the peace we seek. Woman, man, child. Warrior, shifter, Danuja, Native, or magician. We are all equal. I stand before you a woman, strong and proud. I do not fear the road that lies ahead. I stand before you," she moved her hands up and out to her sides palms facing out towards the crowd, "a queen. I will not back down. I will not give up and I will not let any of you either. I will make you mad. I will make you work. And I pray that when our journey comes to an end, I will make you proud." She did take Aslan's hand now and pulled him up to stand beside her, holding their joined hands up in the air. "I stand before you, my brother at my side and promise you a new tomorrow filled with unlimited potential. All I ask is that you join me, join *us,* in making it our new today."

A roar rose in her ears and it took a moment for her to process that it was the cheers of the crowd. They were applauding, some jumping while others hollered and waved. It made her catch her breath once more at the sheer enormity of what they all faced in the days to come.

She prayed that the blood that would be shed soon would fall mostly from the enemy.

Silence descended once more and she turned to see her brother down on one knee beside her, right fist over his heart. One by one every member of the crowd joined him but what stunned her was that her mates and sister did as well.

"Long live the Queen," he yelled and with a deafening roar the crowd took up the chant.

Wilhelm was not happy with the way things were going. The Danuja giant had not been broken and now was free though his power was still somewhat limited thanks to Wilhelm's spell. Two more of his men were dead thanks to that bitch who even now was trying to take her mother's place as queen. She would have to die, and the sooner the better as far as he was concerned. He could hear the chant of 'long live the queen' from where he hid and sneered with contempt.

"We'll see whose life is longer," he scoffed and turned to head deep into his lair once more, plots already forming in his mind. The battle was only just beginning.

SHIFTER'S DELIGHT

Dedication

To all the fans who continue to purchase my books and share their joy with me. It is because of you that I am able to write. Your love and encouragement are deeply appreciated.

To Melissa, your help makes my work so much better!

Prologue

She was in love. Or at least she had been before the truth had slammed into her with brutal force. He didn't love her, never had. She had been nothing but a diversion for him, someone soft and willing to pass the time with. And she would be forever grateful that she hadn't divulged her secret to him in the afterglow of great sex. For really that is all it had amounted to. Great sex. And that only made her hurt more now that she knew who he was, what he was. And the things he had done.

Lydia hurried to the room where the twin infants that she was nursemaid to awaited. She prayed that she was in time to stop her queen—no her best friend—who happened to be queen, from making a mistake that would wound them all. Someone had to talk some sense into Queen Ona. Someone had to stop her from going to meet Wilhelm, from walking into what was sure to be her death.

Lydia stopped just inside the door as she heard Ona talking to her daughter Aurora. Her eyes filled with tears as she realised her friend was telling her children goodbye.

"You'll begin the salvation of us all. Your blood shall start what his shall finish. When the time is right, you shall draw the sword and become the strength as is your birthright. You'll grow strong and smart. You'll laugh. And you'll love. You'll lose and you'll find. My heart breaks for all you will face. But rest assured that you will not stand alone. Time will bring you all together. And a common enemy shall bind you tight." Ona bent low to place a kiss on her daughter's brow. "You are my daughter. Know my strength, know my love, and call upon them as you need."

"Please don't go," Lydia begged as she walked into the room.

"I have no choice," Ona told her.

"He will kill you," Lydia stated.

"Yes," Ona agreed. "He will."

"Then don't do this," Lydia cried. "We need you."

"If I do not go, he will kill us all," Ona said and Lydia fought tears once more as her friend's gaze went back to her children.

"We will fight for you," Lydia declared.

"It is my choice," Ona said softly. "And I choose to do what is best for everyone. The death of one to save many."

"How can your death be good for anyone?" Lydia cried.

"You will see," Ona said. "But first I must ask something of you."

"Anything," Lydia promised and meant it more than anything else in the world. "I will do anything."

"I was hoping you would say that," Ona said. "I ask the most important task of you. Take my daughter and flee back to your people. He must not find her until the time is right."

Lydia held her sobs back admirably as she nodded. She was humbled by the great task that Ona ask of her, the task of raising her daughter, the future queen.

"And Lydia," Ona reached out to place her hand on Lydia's still flat tummy. "He must not know of the child you carry. All of your lives depend on it."

Lydia gasped. How did Ona know of the child she carried? How could she when Lydia had only just realised herself? Her adoration of Wilhelm was well known to her friend, so that Ona knew it was his was understandable. She placed her hand across her stomach. She would have two children to watch over and protect. And she would see that neither knew a day without love.

"When you hear the commotion you must take up Aurora and flee," Ona told Lydia. "They will head here first. His guard. They must only find Aslan. They will guard my son with their lives. But you must be gone before they get here."

Lydia nodded her agreement and Ona reached out to take her into a fierce hug. "Sister of my heart, know that what you do for me is the greatest gift of all. Guard her and raise her as a sister to your child. They will need the bond to conquer the battles that lie ahead."

She knew the questions that hovered on her tongue shone in her eyes, knew that Ona could see the struggle she waged to keep them unspoken. And the confidence her friend had in her was overwhelming.

"Tell her of me. The woman you knew, not the queen. Tell her of my love, of my joy at her birth. Tell her she has my eyes, my heart, and when the time is right she will know the power of her birth. Prepare her, train her, but do not raise her to be queen. That is a journey she must begin on her own. She may know of me but not of this place or anything that lies here. Promise me that."

"I promise," Lydia swore. And it was one she would keep. Aurora would know of Ona, the woman, her mother. But she would not know of the title her mother held, or that she had a twin brother. As soon as Aurora knew that she would leave and Lydia would not be able to protect her then.

The hardest moment of her life was watching her best friend walk away from her, knowing that she would never see Ona alive again. She wanted to leap out, throw herself in front of Ona and beg once more for her to find another way. But she couldn't. She had to trust that Ona was doing what she must. And Lydia had to take care of Aurora.

She walked quickly to Aslan and looked down upon him.

"My beautiful baby boy, I will miss you every day." She reached into her pocket and removed some scissors using them to snip a tiny piece of his hair. "I take a part of you with me for I could never be whole without it. You will grow and thrive and I pray that the choices made for you in this hour bring you to a joyous place. I pray that you grow strong and proud and that you feel the mantle of your mother's love always." Her tears splashed on him. "I pray that you will forgive me for leaving you and taking her. I pray that your anger will not control you. I pray that he will not be able to turn you against your own." She scooped him up and hugged him to her inhaling his unique scent and praying that she never forgot it. "When the time is right you will send for me. When the time is right, I will come. I pray that you know when you see me that I have only ever loved you." She kissed him softly on the brow and placed him down once more. It broke her heart to know that she had to leave him behind.

She turned to Aurora and bundled her quickly before using rope to tie the bundle to her chest. She would have to shift when she was far enough away and she would need Aurora tied securely to her. It was the only way that they would get away fast enough before he sent soldiers after them.

Lydia walked to the door, a cloak thrown over them to hide that Aurora was with her. She glanced back to where Aslan lay content for the moment. And she prayed.

May the goddess have mercy on them all.

Chapter One

Lynx gave a weary sigh. So much had happened in the last few days. Her sister Aurora being kidnapped and finding out that Aurora was the long lost daughter of the murdered queen. Which made Aurora the new queen. Then discovering that King Aslan felt Lynx's momma Lydia had kidnapped Aurora. And that was only the tip of the iceberg.

She rubbed absently at her side remembering vividly the searing pain that had ripped through her when one of Wilhelm's men had stabbed her. She closed her eyes and recalled with perfect clarity the exact moment.

Someone stabbed her and with a roar that shook the trees she shifted back to human form. There was a searing, burning pain and the smell of her blood reached her nostrils. She looked up to see the man who had done this to her, to curse him. And was awed.

A man stepped forward, a mountain of a man. Her breath caught in her lungs as she took him in. Seven feet tall with long brown hair that hung in braids to his shoulders. And the most amazing eyes she'd ever seen, a soft golden shade. He was truly beautiful and powerful. With no effort he picked up the man who had stabbed her and threw him from them.

The king said something to her but she was totally focussed on the tall man as he knelt beside her and held his hands out.

"May I?" he asked and his voice was melodic as the sweetest music. She thought he wanted to check her wound which was still burning with pain. Instead he held his hand over her flesh and closed his eyes in concentration. Lynx felt heat move from him to her and watched in amazement as her wound began to heal. Muscle and tissue mended before her eyes and the flesh began to close back up. More importantly the pain was leaving.

Everything happened so quick after that. She could have sworn she heard Aurora called queen but that couldn't be right. Then they were heading towards the castle. She felt woozy and the next thing she knew the giant who had healed her lifted her high against his chest and carried her. She listened and learned.

His name was Micah, he was Danuja and his brother was being held captive somewhere on their island. He was worried for his brother who had been missing for months and about a plot that had reached his land that had to do with a threat to the king. What interested her most though was the way the scent of his skin made her mouth water. She wanted to taste him, to lick him from head to toe. So… She flirted, squeezed his neck and rubbed against him. But Micah didn't respond. She might have thought he wasn't interested if it wasn't for his increased breathing and the visible pulse she could see in his neck.

So she tortured them both by leaning up to whisper in his ear making sure her chest rubbed against his.

"I'm very grateful for what you did for me, Micah," she whispered letting her breath wash over him.

"My pleasure," he assured her.

"I've never had anyone heal me like that before," she whispered again and she wondered if he could feel how hard her nipples were. The man was seriously sexy.

"It is what I do," he said again and she felt him shift his arms as if to move her away from him. She just tightened her arms around his neck and rubbed closer.

Micah took her into the room that was indicated as hers for while she was here and laid her gently on the big bed. She kept her arms around his neck long enough to give him a soft kiss on the cheek just inches from his lips.

"Thank you so much, Micah," she told him. "I'd be in a lot of pain if it wasn't for you."

He caught his breath and for just a moment she met his eyes and saw the desire he felt. But it was quickly hidden and he pulled firmly away. "Anytime," he said and walked away from her shutting the door behind him.

That was the first time she met Micah and she had felt something for him from that very first moment. There was just something about a person saving your life that created an undeniable bond. But that was only the beginning of the chaos that was now her emotional state. There was also Merced, Micah's brother who had been held captive by Wilhelm.

She smiled as she recalled how she had shifted into the smaller domesticated cat form and followed one of the castle servants on her search for Micah's brother. They had gone down a hidden staircase in the kitchen to a dark area beneath the castle that reeked of the smell of blood and death. Merced had also awed her from the start.

She almost peed when a hand appeared out of nowhere and she was grabbed by the scruff of her neck.

"Well, what have we here?" a voice said and she was lifted against a massive chest, secure but not hurt by any means. "A pretty pussy to pass the time with."

Somehow those words sent a chill through her, as if the man holding her tabby form knew that she was not merely a cat and that the petting he wanted was more towards her human form.

She peered up at him and was shocked to see a face so similar to Micah's that this could be none other than his brother. The resemblance was to the point that if she did not know better she would swear it was Micah. Only this man was even taller than Micah's seven feet, broader of shoulder and yet not as strong on the inside as Micah. She remembered that he had been missing for a good six months at least. What exactly had Wilhelm been doing to this man?

"So what should I do with such a pretty little kitty?" he murmured and she meowed.

He laughed and the sound was deep and rich. His eyes were not quite as golden as Micah's. No, his eyes had dark brown flecks in them. His smile was just as warm and inviting though. His hair was longer but she didn't know if it was by choice or circumstance. Either way it looked really good on him. It was hard to judge from her position against his chest but it looked a long way down to the floor. She would bet he was at least an inch or two taller than Micah's seven foot frame.

Man she was as bad as her sister Aurora. Lynx had thought she had it bad for Micah but, hell, she was just as hot for his brother. Even as a cat she was content to lie snug against his chest. If he continued to stroke her with his fingers she just might sprawl and purr…after shifting back into human form. Lord, she just needed to have sex which was a laugh and a half.

The one time she had managed to sneak off with another shifter to learn what all the thrill was about she had only got so far before her wonderful mother had interrupted them. But before that interruption she had found out just how well it felt to have a tongue bath in all the right places. She had still been in the thrall of her first orgasm when her mother appeared. Mamma may have prevented her from popping the proverbial cherry but she hadn't prevented her from thoroughly enjoying the full extent of foreplay.

His fingers stroked along her fur again and she really wanted to know his name because heaven help her she was going to be moaning it soon.

He knelt down and placed her gingerly on the cool floor before standing and melding back into the shadows. She could feel him but could no longer see him. She wondered if that was some form of magic within him or within the place.

"Scamper home," he murmured far above her. "Before the bogey man shows and you never get away." His voice was sad now and hearing the change made her sad as well.

Two different men, brothers even and she could get neither of them out of her head. She wanted answers, knew that soon she would demand them. But for now she went over everything in her head and tried to see what, if anything she might have missed. She'd been in such a hurry to get back to Micah and let him know that she had found Merced. Her excitement had her practically bouncing the entire way to his room. And that night, well that night was etched in her memory.

He'd yelled at her for going off on her own. Made her feel foolish and child-like which only served to make her angry. Then he had deflated her anger by finally thanking her only to confuse the hell out of her by telling her they would wait through the night and go after Merced in the morning. He wanted a plan and she'd told him that Merced was fine. He took her at her word.

He put her in his bed and told her to sleep while he took a spot on the floor in front of the door to the room. She'd been restless, unable to shut her mind or body off to find the sleep he felt they both needed. So she'd waited until she thought him slumbering and then made her way to the door having no option but to go over his prone form. But Micah hadn't been sleeping and what she'd felt that night was a first for her.

She stretched one long leg over him one arm already reaching for the door when she heard the deep sigh. She turned so that she looked towards his face when she almost screamed. His hands came up and grabbed behind her knees and the next thing she knew she was flat on her back with Micah looming over her with her knees locked over his elbows. His hands were braced beside her shoulders and he leaned in keeping her completely under his power.

It was Lynx's turn to sigh. She was hot as hell for Micah. In this position she could feel every hard angle of him and she wanted more. Without thought she leaned up and nipped soft kisses along his jaw. He tensed for a minute and then her legs were sliding down his arms to fall sprawled at her sides and he was lying fully on top of her. His mouth found the pulse point in her throat and explored there.

He was naked from the waist up and Lynx ran her hands over every inch of bare flesh that she could. He was so broad, the hair on his chest more wiry and coarse than what she had felt before when playing with men from her shifter tribe. Micah was different and she loved it, wanted to feel more of him.

His mouth moved down her throat to her chest and then her shirt was being tugged up. No time to prepare, just Micah's hot mouth closing over her nipple sucking deep and hard. She arched up from the floor, trying to muffle the cry that wanted to pour from her lips. His big hand cupped her other breast, his fingers pulling and tugging at that nipple. One hard thigh rode high between her legs and she could feel the magnificent length of his cock against her inner thigh.

Micah was a big man and she wasn't talking about the fact that he was seven feet tall. She wanted him, wanted to feel him buried deep inside her. She rubbed wantonly against him and she knew he must be able to feel the heat and wetness of her sex on his thigh. He groaned and his mouth left her nipple with a popping sound before he licked his way over to the other one.

Her hands clawed at his shoulders trying to hold him closer, trying to pull him up her body so that his hard cock would lie where she wanted it and she could feel his lips on hers. She wanted to know the sensual feel of his kiss, to feel his tongue stroking against hers. She wanted to grip his hips with her legs and rub her hot sex along the length of his. She wanted desperately.

But Micah moved further down his lips trailing a path along her stomach. With ease he pushed her pants down and his mouth was at her pussy. His tongue slid between the plumped lips and she could hear the pleasure in his voice as her taste filled his mouth. His chest on her knees kept her from moving, kept her at his mercy.

One big hand stretched along her stomach so that his fingers could still torture the nipple of one breast while the other spread the lips of her pussy for his further exploration. His tongue was a torment as it glided up and around her swollen clitoris only to trail back down and rim her opening. Again and again he traced this path until she was ready to scream.

Then his tongue was inside her fucking her channel while he used one finger to rub circles on her clit. She tried to keep the moans she could no longer contain low but the pleasure coursing through her was like none she had ever felt before.

"Micah," Lynx breathed his name and his head came up to look at her. His mouth was wet with her juices and his eyes were so golden that they looked like twin suns. "Micah," she said, again unsure of herself in this new experience.

His nostrils flared and his eyes seemed to glow impossibly brighter before his head lowered once more to gorge on her. His tongue and fingers did a wicked erotic dance on her pussy that had her climbing towards what she knew would be pleasure like none she had felt before. A finger filled her pussy pressing high and rubbing in a spot that had her throttling back a scream as orgasm crashed over her.

The finger rubbed for just a moment longer before slipping free only to be replaced by his tongue. His mouth softened and he eased her through orgasm. She was soft and pliant and feeling more than ready to have him ease up her body and slide his cock inside her. But he eased up to her side and turned her so that he was behind her holding her against his chest.

With a softly whispered, "go to sleep," he stroked his hand down her length relaxing her further. And despite her resistance Lynx fell asleep.

The next morning he'd been gone when she awoke, already off to plan with the others leaving her behind. She'd rushed to catch up and managed to arrive just in time to watch her sister fighting with two of Wilhelm's men. Aurora was amazing to watch.

That was when she got her first true glimpse of Wilhelm. He was nothing like what she had envisioned and yet there was a distinct taint of evil around him. He'd taken his men and left and they had gone to Aslan's war room to plan a course of action. Her heart had stopped when Aurora said she wanted to bring Lydia to the castle. Lynx didn't want her mother any place that might put her in danger.

But Aurora made a good argument. Lydia must have knowledge that they needed and thus it made it imperative that she be brought to the castle. King Aslan assured Lynx that her mamma would be welcomed and protected and there was nothing to do but agree. With that matter settled they had moved to discussing her search the previous night and how to go about rescuing Merced.

That one moment was really where everything changed for her.

Chapter Two

In less than an hour they were making their way through the halls to the kitchen where Lynx knew a secret door was. She prayed with all her heart that they were not too late to save Merced. Things seemed way to quiet and it made her wonder if Wilhelm had a spy closer in their mist than even they knew. Honestly other than Aslan, none of the others knew the men the king counted as his most trusted. And looking at how well Aslan had been played as a pawn by Wilhelm it made one stop and question.

They had spent precious minutes divining the best course of action and waiting for Aslan's most trusted warriors to arrive. First to arrive were Piers and Seer. They were both tall with brown wavy hair and big green eyes, though Piers' were darker. They were quick to greet Aslan with a warm embrace. And Aslan was quick to smile and return their hug of friendship.

Next were Lake and Lincoln, both golden haired charmers. Lake had blue eyes while Lincoln's were nearly black. The same laughs and hugs were exchanged. From what Lynx could tell the bond was especially tight between Aslan, Piers and Seer. They all greeted her with warm smiles taking her hand between theirs and giving it a firm squeeze. They seemed intrigued by the three shifters in the room and it put Lynx at ease.

Once the greetings and introductions were out of the way they had filled the warriors in on their discoveries and plans. Lynx knew that Aslan still held hope that Wilhelm wasn't to blame for everything but it didn't appear that his closest warriors held his hope. It seemed that perhaps they knew more than Aslan and just maybe had kept it from him out of an unwillingness to hurt him. But they had been wrong and now Merced could be one of the many that paid for that loyalty. In blood.

Lynx moved quickly through the halls towards where she knew the door was. It was easy to see that the warriors were only letting her lead because they had been unaware of where the entrance was. They seemed to think that she should be behind them. She almost laughed at such an absurd notion. She could kill them with ease and skill if she so choose to shift. Even the smallest of cat forms was deadly when needed.

Lynx pushed through the door and entered the kitchen. As she moved around the people grew deathly quiet. She wasn't sure if it was to see the king and queen in their kitchen or because perhaps they all knew what the party with her was searching for. She could sense their fear, smell it hovering in the air. She let her eyes search doing her best to find the door. Where the hell had it been? It was definitely well hidden.

Finally the young girl Lynx had followed the previous day stepped forward, shy and obviously nervous. Lynx glanced at the girl and smiled. Then she shifted into a small tabby cat that she knew the girl would recognise.

"It was you who went down the stairs with me," the girl exclaimed and picked Lynx up and gave her a quick squeeze. Suddenly the girl squeaked and dropped Lynx back to the floor. "I'm so sorry. I didn't mean to harm you."

"No harm done," Nado reassured the girl. "Shifters are a resilient lot."

"You are the one who delivers the tray to the prisoner below," Micah said as he stepped forward.

The girl gasped and backed up. "How did you escape him?"

Micah's feral expression softened at the girl's fear. "I am not he but I seek him, and quickly before it is too late."

"You know where the door is?" Aslan stepped forward now and claimed the girl's attention. Lynx was annoyed by the conversation. *Just find the damn door.* Time was running out.

The girl nodded and crossed the kitchen by the stove. She pulled a cabinet open and with a press of her fingers a panel slid open inside. A staircase was revealed that descended into the depths of the castle. Lynx, who had maintained her tabby form, shot through the opening and disappeared into the darkness beyond. She heard Domi's unmistakable roar and knew that he followed close on her heels.

She came to the hallway and immediately turned to follow it to where she remembered Merced was being held. She stopped at the spot where his hand had reached out the night before and tried in vain to pass through without his aid. But she couldn't. She shifted to her human form. Domi and Nado were with her.

"Where is he?" Nado asked as he shifted to human form.

"Behind this wall," she said. "I've been through it once, yesterday, but I don't know how to pass through it now."

"There must be some way," Nado said and began moving around gently touching the wall as Lynx was but he had no more luck than she did at finding a way in.

Micah came flying down the corridor towards them and with a yell he leapt right through the wall in front of their eyes.

Lynx recoiled when Micah's cry of pain and anguish filled the air. "Micah," she screamed and turned to Nado. "Follow him!"

Both she and Nado moved back to do just that but Nado was quicker. With a roar he ran forward where Micah had gone through. Lynx could sense something, as if someone were trying to whisper to her not to try and follow.

Lynx yelled, "No!" but it was too late. Nado hit the wall full force and then with an explosion of light was flung across the hall to land crumpled on the floor. Lynx prayed to the goddess that he was okay. Otherwise she did not want to be around when her sister got here.

"He will live." The voice filled her head and she closed her eyes in relief. It was undoubtedly Micah's and she could feel how hard it was for him to make the connection with her. *"Merced is unconscious but weak. I must go into a trance to try and heal him. I am a healer, sort of like a holy man among my people, but even I may not be strong enough to heal him. Domi can hear me too in his animal form."* Lynx turned towards the panther and saw that he was indeed hearing the same as she was. *"Find the way in. We will be waiting."* And then nothing but silence.

Footsteps sounded and Lynx turned in time to see two men moving towards her and Domi who was still in panther form. She knew it would be easier for him to sense what if any damage Nado had sustained while in his animal form. They had Micah's word that Nado was okay but okay could mean different things to different people. There was a link between the two panthers that always made other shifters wonder if they were not related by blood.

The men moved towards them quietly as if they thought she and Domi were unaware of their presence. She let them get close, let them think they had the upper hand.

"Well, what shifter trash do we have here?" one of them sneered as swords were drawn and pointed at them. Goddess bless the stupidity of those who had never actually battled with a shifter. Thoughts were tumbling through her mind when one of them had the audacity to kick Nado.

She bared her teeth in a snarl as she began automatically shifting into her favourite fear invoking form. The lion. Mightiest of all cats, often thought to be a king among beasts. Domi had the one who had kicked Nado cornered against one side of the hall and she easily backed the other to the wall just a foot or so away.

Domi was snarling and in danger of ripping the man's throat out for what he had done. So Lynx did what she knew would get her sister's attention. The warriors were checking the cells back the way they had come and this would get all their attention.

She lifted her lions head and gave a roar that echoed and thundered through the hallway. The man in front of her whimpered and the scent of fear seeped from his skin like stale sweat to add to the stench already in the air. Opening her mouth wide she leaned up closer to him and let out another might roar.

The man cringed and Lynx could hear the thunder of running feet moving towards them as the others headed for her and Domi.

Aurora was the first to reach them and Lynx could feel her sister's tension as she stopped to kneel beside Nado. He was still silent and unmoving but Lynx could easily sense that he was merely knocked unconscious. But what she couldn't sense was what was going on beyond the invisible wall that Micah and Merced were behind. And now there was no sound. That silence unnerved her and had her praying to the goddess as she never had before.

With a great warrior's cry Aurora flew across the space towards them and Lynx wanted to laugh as she felt the fear grow in the two men. Her sister was truly a sight to behold. With an amazing leap Aurora was airborn with her sword raised high above her head. Lynx planned to frame this moment in her mind. The very power that emanated from her sister was breathtaking.

The sword swished through the air and with a clang of steel it severed through the neck of the man Domi had cornered. The man before her gave a high keening wail that made her want to reach out and swipe him dead with one mighty paw. He dropped the weapon he had been holding at his side and fell to his knees begging her sister for his life.

Lynx followed Domi's lead and backed up, shifting to human form as Aslan joined Aurora. Lynx was anxious to breach the wall and get to Micah and Merced.

Aslan motioned to the man and his fallen companion. "We need these men to find out all we can about this."

"It only takes one to talk," Aurora replied before taking her blade and laying it beside the neck of the man Lynx had recently guarded. "And I pray the answers you have are the right ones. For your sake."

"Yes! Yes! Yes!" the man screamed, sobbing and managing to look quite pathetic. What a waste of human flesh as far as Lynx was concerned. She doubted any information was worth saving him but then she was not queen and luckily didn't have to make that decision.

Aurora turned towards her and Domi and demanded "What happened here?"

Domi had moved once more to Nado and Lynx felt jealous of the look that passed between Domi and Aurora. There was so much conveyed without words as if they were already so connected that they could read one another's thoughts.

Lynx stepped in, wanting to bring their attention to what was her main concern at the moment. Micah and Merced.

"There is some type of force field here," and she indicated what she knew the others would see as just more wall obscured by darkness.

"The wall?" Aurora asked.

"No, and yet made to appear as such," Lynx stated. "Micah was able to pass through and once I was able to as well," she swallowed hard and when she looked up it was with tears in her eyes. Nado was on the floor because of her. "Which is why I told Nado to follow Micah. I thought he would be able to get through as well. But when I passed through it was as a tabby and I was in the arms of a Danuja."

"Merced," Aurora stated and Lynx nodded. "So we have found him and now lost Micah as well?"

"Micah was able to pass through but cannot get back to us. His magic isn't that strong. He is a healer, sort of like a holy man for his people. Merced would be able to but he is too weak. Micah has gone into some kind of a trance to try and heal Merced. We haven't heard from him in a while and I am worried for them both." Lynx knew that her sister could sense her emotions which were so close to the surface right now. She had strong feelings for Micah and just maybe for Merced as well. Enough that she definitely wanted them alive and well, able to explore possibilities with her. She prayed they could get both of the Danuja free of Wilhelm's prison.

"You," Aurora turned back to the remaining man. "Tell me what you know of this magic. Now. And it had best be useful."

"Tis Danuja magic," the man stammered. "Placed by one to contain one."

"And?" Aurora said making a point to lift her sword, the blade still stained red.

He swallowed hard. "There is some type of box set high to the top that holds the cell in place. Only by removing it will it cease."

"If I have to prompt you one more time you will lose a limb," Aurora promised. "You do not need those to answer questions."

"At the top," he squealed pointing his finger up high to the ceiling just above the wall. "You can't see the box but you can see where the wall appears just a bit darker in the one spot. That is what you are aiming for."

Lynx glanced at the spot and saw what he was talking about. She might be able to reach it if she shifted back into animal form but she wasn't sure if she could miss hitting the magic field that surrounded it. Her frustration was growing. Then Piers stepped forward removing a small dagger with a wicked curve from his belt. Taking careful aim he threw it with speed and complete accuracy.

There was a crackle and a pop and the wall disappeared revealing the prone shapes of two huge men. Micah and Merced. Lynx yelled and ran to them. They had to be all right.

Chapter Three

Lynx hurried to the two men. Micah was weak, his pulse so soft it took her twice to find it. Merced did not appear to be breathing at all. Without thought she tilted his head back, opened his mouth and pinched his nose. Leaning in she sealed her mouth to his and exhaled blowing her breath into him. Three times she did this before he gasped and finally breathed on his own.

His beautiful golden eyes with flecks of brown opened slowly to greet her. Sensing that he would be fine she turned to Micah which was easy since she knelt between them.

"Micah," she said softly. "Wake up. We still have things to talk about remember?" She would discuss whatever he wanted, her wandering ways or anything, if only he would open his eyes.

"You gave me breath," Merced sounded awed by this as he sat up beside her.

"Yes," she nodded still focused on Micah. "But your brother is still weak. Is there anything you can do to help him?"

Merced stared at her for a moment before turning to his brother. He inhaled deeply and leaned into his brother's face before exhaling. She watched in amazement as a golden glow seemed to leave his mouth and sink into Micah's skin. Within mere seconds Micah was opening his eyes and sitting up beside her. Without thought Lynx launched herself at him raining kisses over his face.

"Micah," she smiled. "I thought I had lost you."

"Not so easily little cat," he whispered.

"You should not be so foolish brother," Merced interrupted them and Lynx would swear that she heard anger in his voice. "You almost lost your life and yet still it would not have saved me."

"And yet here you are?" Micah stated.

"No thanks to you," Merced replied. "It was your little cat that breathed life into me."

Micah gasped and looked down at Lynx. "She breathed into you?" he asked and she was getting confused.

"Yes," Merced said and she could almost feel Micah deflating like a balloon. It must have shown on his face as well for Merced's voice softened with his next words.

"She did not know," Merced said and placed his hand on Micah's shoulder to give it a squeeze.

"It matters not," Micah said and easing her from his lap he stood. "The law is clear. What is to be is to be."

"Micah," Merced helped Lynx to her feet as Micah stood.

"Good to have you back brother," was all that Micah said as he turned to the rest of the group leaving Lynx standing with Merced.

"What just happened here?" she asked quietly looking up at the big man.

"It seems that you and I will be having a talk little cat," Merced said. "But first there are other things to see to."

She stood alone for a moment watching the ones around her. The joy on her sister's face as Nado sat up and embraced Aurora. The way Domi's face tilted into a half grin as Nado said something. The stance of the warriors that surrounded them and the look of pleasure on Aslan's face as he took in his sister's happiness. Then she focused on her Danuja. Brothers reunited and yet there seemed such distance between them. What had just happened? She knew that it had something to do with her and breathing into Merced. She wondered how long she would have to wait before finding out.

She stood to the side between her sister's mates Domi and Nado as Aurora gave her first speech as queen. It was amazing to witness. Her sister's words were inspiring and Lynx could feel the pride in her heart as she watched the crowd's faces. They loved Aurora. She was exactly what everyone needed. And when Aslan bent to his knee it was only natural that Lynx did as well. What surprised her was that Domi and Nado did as well as her Danuja Micah and Merced.

She wanted to speak to them, one or both to get to the bottom of what had happened. All she had done was revive Merced and now Micah acted as if she belonged to his brother. It made no sense to her. But she was damn sure that she would have answers by night's end.

A crowd of warriors gathered around Aurora, and Domi and Nado stepped up beside her so Lynx took that moment to slip away through the crowd to the room she was staying in. She needed a moment alone to centre her thoughts and plot her next move. But it wasn't meant to be.

"Time to talk, little cat," Merced said as he pushed his way into the room behind her. She must have been lost in thought to have missed the fact that he'd followed her.

"Where is Micah?" she asked as she tried to look beyond the big man. Micah and Merced where big guys, both easily seven feet in height. She felt positively tiny in comparison.

"It is only I for this talk," Merced said and motioned towards the bed behind her. "Please have a seat."

She lifted her eyebrow at him. "I prefer to stand for now. And why is Micah not a part of this talk?"

"He has chosen to remove himself for now," was the only reply Merced gave.

"And I thought I meant more to him after the other night," she said wondering just what kind of game these two brothers were playing.

"I'm not sure just what you shared with my brother," Merced stated. "I can tell that you have not mated with him as your aura is still almost only you with no trace of him."

"My aura?" she interrupted.

"It is the ring of life that surrounds you," Merced replied. "When you are mated as your sister is, your life-force blends with that of your mates. That link provides a new stronger power."

"I don't understand any of that," Lynx said with a shake of her head. "So I'll just have to take your word for it. But you did say that it was almost all me with no trace of him. What else do you see?" She meant who but wasn't going to say that. Who else other than Micah could her life-force or whatever be linked with?

"Me," was the quiet reply that had her eyes jerking up to meet his.

"You?" she whispered suddenly feeling light-headed and moving to sit quickly on the side of the bed. "Why would it be you? We have not touched."

Merced looked sad for a moment. "But we have, little cat. We have. Our life forces merged when you breathed your essence into me."

"You weren't breathing," she stated, anger filling her. "What was I suppose to do? Just leave you?"

"I was in a trance," he began but she cut him off.

"So was Micah but I could see that he was breathing," she yelled.

"Do you know anything of the Danuja?" he asked.

"Micah is the first that I have met," she said. "I have heard of the powers that you can hold. Healers, mystics, sorcerers of great magic. But only stories."

"Micah is what you would call a healer," Merced stated. "His magic is good, pure. He is also a reader which means that he can see your life-force and know if you are telling truth or lie, if you are ill or close to death."

"And you?" she asked almost afraid to know, somehow sensing that she didn't want to know.

"I am what is called Damikan in Danuja," he said.

"Damikan?" she repeated.

He nodded. "I am more but my power is limited in my weakened state."

She took in the powerful male before her. This was a weakened state? "More?"

"That is unimportant right now," he said. "What I want to share with you is important though and it has to do with you and I."

"What about you and I?" she questioned.

"In Danuja culture there are certain things that can only be shared between mates," he began. "And once they are shared, a link, or bond, is formed between the two."

"And?" she prompted when he stopped. "What does that have to do with you and me?"

"One of those things is the mating ritual," he stated and looked down, not meeting her eyes. It made her want to laugh. Would he be so uncomfortable during the act? "Not just the mating of bodies but that of mouths as well."

So that was why Micah had not kissed her. She had wanted his kiss and he had kept it from her, perhaps to save her from stepping into what she didn't understand. She caught just the tail end of what Merced was saying but it was enough to have her head whipping up.

"What did you say?" she demanded.

"I said like what we shared," he repeated softly.

"I heard that part," she informed him. "It's the first part that I need you to repeat."

He gave a weary sigh and finally looked at her. "I said that the other form of mating is the blending of souls or spirits and this is achieved by sharing your breath or life essence with another. Just as you did with me."

"But I didn't know," she stated shaking her head. "I didn't know."

"I understand that and as such I will not hold you to anything," he smiled and nodded turning from her so that she could not see his face, his eyes, his feelings. "But I will warn you that such a sharing is sacred among the Danuja and especially to someone thought as a holy man."

"Micah?" she must have breathed his name aloud because she saw the sudden tension in Merced's body.

"Yes, Micah," was the terse response and she sensed that she had angered him in some way. Without turning to her he moved quickly back to the door and pulled it open.

"Now if you will excuse me, I have much to do." And with that he was gone.

If she would excuse him? Oh, hell no! You didn't just come in and tell someone basically that you were mated and then leave. And if he was more than Micah and this meant so much to Micah then what did it mean to Merced? She had wanted answers but Merced had filled her with more questions. And she'd be damned if she waited around for one of them to follow her again. She knew where Micah's room was. She remembered it well.

Throwing her door open she moved down the hall towards his room and the unmistakably angry voices that were coming from inside. Shifting to enhance her hearing she pressed her tabby ear against the door.

"Do you love her?" Merced's voice carried and it was angry.

"It does not matter," was the reply and Micah's voice lacked the energy that she associated with him.

"Of course it matters," Merced thundered. "Everything matters."

"She has mated with you," Micah said quietly, almost too quietly for her to pick up.

"And yet she hasn't," Merced said. "It is not me she wants. It is not my name she whispers."

"And yet it doesn't matter," Micah insisted. "I am Danuja and am bound by that. Her breath is in you and that is all that is of importance now."

"Do you think this is what I would have wished for you?" Merced sounded anguished. "Do you think I can't feel your pain, the way your heart aches for her?"

"Do I love her?" Micah yelled. "Do I wish that it was me she breathed into? Yes, damn you I do. But what good will that wish do me? Where will that get me? What does that knowledge do for you? Does it make things better or worse for both of us?"

"And in this we are both screwed, my brother," Merced stated with a laugh that contained no humour. "I find myself mated to a woman that I cannot claim. One that my brother is in love with. With all my power I cannot change what now is. The fates have conspired and it is I that they laugh at."

"Woo her," Micah said. "Teach her to know you and she won't be able to do anything but love you. She is a woman worthy of the Damikan. She will inspire great love in all who meet her."

"And what of you my brother?" Merced asked with a sadness that clenched around Lynx's heart. "What is to become of you? Do you move on to someone else? Do you have to watch me every day with the woman you love?"

"That is more than I can do," Micah stated. "Even for you. And it is more than you should have to bear. She will forget me. I was but a moment in her life. You can be her life."

"What did you share with her?" Merced asked.

"A moment," Micah replied. "Just one incredible moment. Do you love her Merced?"

A long sigh filled the air. "Perhaps," he answered. "Her spirit already fills me. I could love her but it is not her wish."

What if it was her wish? What if she did want Merced? And why did she have to choose between them? Why couldn't she follow in Aurora's footsteps, in the footsteps of many of the classes of people on their island home? Why couldn't she mate with both men? And why the hell were they having this conversation without her?

Chapter Four

She shifted back to human form and burst into the room. Micah and Merced were on opposite sides of the room. The tension was even thicker on this side of the door but Lynx no longer cared. They were not allowed to make decisions about her life without including her. And it was best to make them aware of that now. Somehow she had sealed her fate when she had used her breath to revive Merced. That was fine. She was a big girl and she would accept that. But not without making Micah a part of it as well. In her opinion the fact that Micah had tasted her pussy was more of a tie than sharing air with Merced. They would just have to accept that.

"You think it's okay to just make all the decisions for me?" she demanded slamming the door behind her. "Do you love her? I'm so sorry brother. Well boo fucking hoo," she stated. "This is my life you two are discussing and deciding and I think I have a say in it as well."

"You will not be held accountable for your actions," Merced stated. "You are unaware of our culture."

"And you know everything about mine?" she asked.

"Yes," both men answered and it threw her for a minute.

"Well good for you," she finally replied. "But you can know all you want about the culture and still not know a person. I am more than my culture. More than their ways and beliefs. I am a woman, a shifter. You cannot classify who I am."

"Touché," Merced answered with a twitch of his lips.

"No one is leaving this room until I get some answers," Lynx stated crossing her arms over her chest and standing before the door. It would have been laughable under other circumstances to think that someone of her stature could keep Micah and Merced in the room if they didn't want to remain. But both men just nodded.

"What is it you seek?" Merced asked.

"Answers," she replied. "Answers filled with truth and honesty. No speaking in riddles or explaining so that I don't understand."

"As you wish," Merced stated.

"And damn it I am not just talking to you," she yelled glaring at Merced before turning to Micah. "I expect you to be a part of this conversation as well Micah."

He inclined his head towards her but did not voice a response and she wanted to go up and smack his chest in frustration.

"What is it that you wish to know, little cat?" Merced asked.

What to pick? There were so many things that she wanted to know, that she needed to know. What did she pick first?

"Who are you Merced?" she asked. "What does the title Damikan mean?"

The brothers looked at one another and Merced gave a weary sigh, his hand going to his forehead and stroking across it as if he was in pain. Finally Micah chose to speak.

"It means that he is king," Micah stated. "And now you are queen."

Holy crap! No way in hell was she a queen. She could feel her head shaking back and forth in denial and couldn't have stopped it if she wanted to.

"I already said that you would not be held responsible for what you didn't know," Merced stated.

"And what about you?" she asked. "Will you be able to mate with another? To choose a more worthy mate as your queen?"

"There is no one more worthy than you," Micah stated and there was anger in his voice. "A woman who places family higher than self. A woman who stands for what is right and just instead of taking the easy path. A woman who has already shed blood for a battle which is not her own."

"It is all of our battle," she replied. "And more blood than mine has and will continue to spill until Wilhelm is stopped." She turned to Merced. "But you have not answered my question."

His hand was on his forehead again. Once more it was Micah who spoke.

"He is king and upholds our laws and customs with no exception. He will take no other as mate," Micah answered.

"And you?" she asked. "Will you take a mate?"

"I believe I already answered that when I said that no woman is more worthy than you," Micah said.

"And what of what we shared the night before?" she asked softly. "Can that mean so little then?"

"Never," he swore while Merced looked on with curiosity and perhaps a bit of sadness. "What we shared is a memory that I will hold in my heart forever."

"Merced is Damikan, or king as you say," she switched gears. "So as his brother what does that make you?"

"My twin," Merced said. "And as such the Damisau of our people."

"Damisau?" she queried.

"He is the religious leader of our people," Merced answered.

"So wait," she said as things began clicking in her head. "Micah said that his people sent someone to speak with Aslan. Why would they send their king?"

"Why ask another to do what you are unwilling to do? And who better to speak with a king than a king?" Merced spoke softly.

"But that makes no sense," Lynx stated baffled. "Who would lead your people if something happened to you? As it obviously did!"

"Micah would," Merced answered.

"And here he is as well," she shook her head. "Who is leading your people now? What if neither of you returned?"

Merced sighed. "Next in line would be Mordecai." He turned to Micah. "I assume he is liaison in our absence?"

Micah nodded.

"I take it Mordecai is a brother?" Lynx asked.

"Yes," they both answered.

"How many brothers do you have?" she asked.

"There are twelve of us," Micah replied.

"Twelve," she exclaimed. Good grief that was a lot of children.

"And we have six sisters," Merced offered.

"Eighteen children?" she could feel how big her eyes were.

"That is not so many in Danuja culture," Merced replied but there was a definite twinkle in his eyes.

"I may be a shifter," Lynx replied. "But I don't plan on having litters of children."

Both of them laughed and it was nice to see. There was a camaraderie between them that she sensed had always been there. At least before she had entered their lives.

"So how quickly do you return to your home and your people?" she asked.

"When the threat is gone," Merced answered. "There is much that Aslan does not know, much that I can make him aware of."

Lynx crossed to him and let her hand reach up to cup his face. "I can only imagine the hell you must have suffered at his hands."

Merced's eyes closed and he seemed to shudder at her touch as if he were starved for it. Six months in a solitary cell suffering who knew what kind of torture. She wanted to hold him, to comfort him. Something had passed between them in that moment when she leaned over and shared her breath, actually even before that during the brief moment he held her to his chest while she was in tabby form. She could feel it when she stood beside him. As if she knew him, his soul, in a way that none other did.

"I would die to keep you from ever knowing," he replied.

"Because I am your mate?" she asked.

"Because you are my life," he replied and she felt humbled by that answer. It was a further glimpse into the Danuja culture.

"I will leave the two of you to talk," Micah said and headed to the door.

"Don't leave," she implored.

"I will not leave the grounds," he said but he refused to look at her, appearing to stare at a spot just over her shoulder. "But for now, this moment, it is best that you two speak alone."

There was pain in his eyes and she wanted to make it go away but there was still so much that she didn't understand. So for now she could only nod as he turned and left the room shutting the door softly behind him.

"What do I do?" she asked Merced, leaning into him. For better or worse she was mated to Merced, a commitment that he obviously took seriously and would honour. But then Micah's words said that he would as well. How could she be the one to tear these two brothers apart? And yet how could she walk away from either one of them?

"I cannot answer that for you," Merced spoke softly. "I would tell you to follow the path your heart leads you on."

"Is that what you plan to do?" she asked already knowing the answer.

"I will follow the path before me," Merced stated and she wanted to smack him.

"You will go on and yet not go on," she said. "In your mind we are mated already and you will not break that vow." When he started to say something she cut him off. "Yes, I know that you will not hold me accountable for my actions since I didn't know. I wish you would," she muttered but he heard her.

"Why would you wish that?" he asked with curiosity.

"Because it would be the coward's way of taking it out of my hands," she whispered shaking her hands. "I've never felt anything like this before, never experienced a pull in two directions. I feel like I am failing miserably and hurting you both in the process."

"We are all accountable for our emotions, our reactions," Merced replied. "The only hurt you feel at the moment is your own."

"Why does it feel like you always answer with a riddle?" she exclaimed. "If I turned to you and asked what you wanted, what would bring you the most joy at this moment, what would you say?"

"Your happiness," he stated softly.

"And that is not acceptable," she almost yelled. "You! I want to know what you would want, Merced. You and Micah both refuse to speak of your needs, desires, or wants."

"It is not our way," he started to say but she cut him off.

"Stop! Just look at me and tell me what you want from me," she pleaded. "I'm so confused right now. I don't know your customs, ways, beliefs. I only know that I did something that mated us. I know that you will let me walk away but you never will. So look me in the eyes and tell me what you would want from me at this moment if you could have anything."

"Let me love you," Merced whispered and once again he managed to put her first. It wasn't "make love to me" or "be with me". It was "let me love you". There was so much conveyed in those words. Need. Desire. Pain. Hope. Feelings rolled off of him and without thought she lifted to him using her hand to pull his head down to her. They were mated so how could it be wrong?

Their lips met and it was so much more than a mere kiss. She'd been kissed before but nothing like this. He was warm and soft and yet the pressure was firm. She could feel her nipples harden where she pressed against him. Even better she could feel the rise of his cock beneath the long robes that both he and Micah wore. She wondered if they wore anything beneath those robes and knew she would find out soon.

The scrape of his teeth against her bottom lip brought her out of her thoughts and had her focussing on his touch. She couldn't feel his breath on her lips and she wanted to ask if he was holding it but she became lost in the other things he was doing. His hands were at her waist and he stroked his palms up under the loose shirt that she wore, inching the material up as his hands climbed. Her hands clenched on his shoulders holding him bent to her. His lips left hers and she arched back exposing her neck for the blazing trail he was taking.

Lips, teeth and tongue worked her flesh and she could hear her breath as she panted with desire. He moved down her throat to the hollow at the base and sucked gently at the skin there. He moved over to the shoulder and bit down on the muscle there, gently but hard enough to send tingles coursing through her.

She cried out, could not contain it, no past experience had prepared her for this moment, for this man. She was suddenly grateful that she had a mother who never left her alone long enough to be with another shifter. It was right for her to share this with Merced. Whether she had meant to or not she had mated him and that made the gift of her first time his by rights. And yet a part of her heart yearned for Micah to be sharing in this moment as well. Even though they had not made love, they had shared an amazing evening.

Merced pulled back and her shirt disappeared over her head. He tossed it to the ground and reached out to cup her breasts in his hands. She had the body of a shifter, long and lean and her breast disappeared in his hands but she could tell by the reverence in his eyes that he liked what he saw. His thumbs rubbed across her aching nipples and she moaned again letting her head fall back on her shoulders.

One hand slipped around to her shoulders and he urged her to follow him across so that he could sit on the side of the bed. She stood between his sprawled thighs with her hands braced on his shoulders. He leaned into her and his mouth closed over one nipple. Warmth surrounded her flesh and she could feel the rub of his tongue. Then he began to suck greedily on her breast and her hands rose to fist in his hair. Streaks of pleasure seemed to flow from her nipple through her breast and down to her pussy which flexed and creamed in anticipation.

He moved to her other nipple and she felt his hands at the waist of her leathers undoing the ties there. He slipped his hands inside and pushed them down over her hips. She helped him by shimmying until they puddled at her feet. She used her feet to slip out of her shoes and then left her pants on top of them. She was completely naked and Merced was still completely clothed.

One of Merced's hands slipped down between her thighs and she heard his sigh as he encountered the wetness there. She was more than ready for him. His fingers moved through her folds until one finger brushed over her clit. She shuddered with desire. His mouth still worked between her breasts and the sensations rioting through her body were making her knees weak. She closed her eyes and then cried out as she felt herself lifted, moving through the air.

Her back made contact with the bed and her eyes flew open. She was sprawled out having flailed as he moved her, her hands wide, palms down, her heels digging into the mattress. Merced looked down at her and moved his hands to the front of the robe he wore. It was a dark brown and fell all the way to his feet, only his arms were bare and even after six weeks of Wilhelm she could still see the muscles bulging there.

His robe fell to the ground. She wasn't sure how it latched as she saw no laces but Merced easily released it so that it fell, revealing every inch of the heaven beneath. His abs were flat and yet still rippled with muscle. His shoulders were broad, his chest a wide plane of muscle spattered with a dusting of dark golden hair. She could see the length and width of his cock defined behind the dark brown clothing he wore. She had never seen anything like the short pants he was wearing.

They were made of the same material as his robe only a shade or two darker. They sat on his hips like her leathers did but only went to the tops of his thighs. They were tight enough that she could easily tell that his cock was proportional to his size and she wanted to lick the wet spot that she knew was his cum. His cock lay at an angle across his hips and she wanted to reach out and lift it up knowing that the head would pop out of the top just ready for her mouth.

But she only made it up onto her elbows before he buried his face between her thighs and with no build up thrust his tongue inside her pussy. With a cry she fell back to the bed gasping. His tongue thrust and licked, fucking her pussy the way she anticipated his cock doing. She lifted her legs so that her heels were outside his shoulders, her legs wide for his touch.

"Yes, little cat," he murmured into her flesh. "Open for me."

He tortured her with pleasure, tormented her with sensation and had her on the edge of ecstasy in moments. His teeth, lips, tongue and fingers were everywhere, working her into a frenzy. She could feel her release within reach.

"Merced," she moaned his name, a whisper, a plea.

His eyes moved up her body to lock with hers and it was as if a bolt of lightning fired between them. Molten gold. That was what his eyes looked like, reminding her of the blinding ball of sun midday. The brown flecks were almost completely gone in this moment and she tried not to think of how similar he looked to Micah. But there was no denying that fact.

She had no idea what he saw in her face, prayed her brief thoughts of Micah were not reflected. But there was no time to be sure as he broke the connection and went back to her pussy, bringing her to an immediate orgasm. It screamed through every cell of her body and she swore she was glowing. It was as if the orgasm shot through every part of her body. Her toes, fingers, nipples, clit, even the hair on her head. It was magic.

Merced groaned as he realised that he had not been able to contain his magic. He had never had that happen before. And the shot that had coursed from him to her had her screaming his name, her body aglow. He could feel his cock begging for release and wanted to feel the firm grip of her pussy hugging his dick, sucking it in as she had his tongue.

But he couldn't. To take her would be to compromise her. And that he would not do. It was bad enough that she knew he could not mate another now. He had Micah to thank for that. Micah. Yet another reason why he could not love her fully. There was something between his brother and his mate and no matter how much Merced wished otherwise there was no changing what was.

One thing was true though. There was no woman more worthy than Lynx. He was already falling in love with his little cat. It would destroy him when the time came to walk away from her. But he would have to respect her enough to do just that. And that meant that he could not take her with his body, with his kiss.

The kiss. That had been torture. It took everything he had to keep his lips firmly closed and not thrust his tongue into her mouth as he had her pussy. He longed for the taste of her kiss, the flicker of her tongue against his own. But they had already shared breath and these other things would only bind them stronger, merge their souls closer. It was okay to fuck, to enjoy the pleasures of the flesh. But never after sharing breath, and it was against their ways to share the intimacy of a soul kiss with any but your mate.

When she lay still and silent he moved up to relax on the bed beside her. At least he could give her pleasure. At least he could love her body the way he wished he could love her. He closed his eyes and sighed. This was a torture far worse than any Wilhelm had come up with, one he might not survive.

Chapter Five

Lynx slowly came back to herself and realised that Merced wasn't taking her, wasn't over her ready to thrust deep inside and bring them both to that pleasure again. She turned her head and saw him reclined on the bed beside her, one knee up, one arm thrown over his face, teeth gritted. She could see the proof of his desire and decided to take matters into her hands. He deserved no less.

She rolled easily and swiftly, figuring that if she didn't move quickly he would try to stop her. So there was no time for teasing, no time to explore as thoroughly as she wanted to. Instead she slipped him quickly free of the cloth and took him in her hand with a firm grip. When he moaned and tried to move away she leaned in and wrapped her lips around the bulbous head of his cock and sucked him as deep as she could.

He stopped moving and she let her eyes move up over his body until they locked with his. Holding his gaze she moved back up his shaft until only the head remained in the confines of her mouth. She worked her tongue up, over and around him, loving the taste that spilled from him. His cock was delicious, like nothing she had ever tasted before. There was no comparison to the salty, sweet flavour that hit her tongue and sent her taste buds to ecstasy. She wanted more and she sucked greedily for it working up and down his shaft.

Merced seemed to lose his control. One big hand reached out to touch her. It was a gentle caress and when she met his gaze again it was to see softness and awe in his eyes. Was it possible to love someone you didn't really know? Was it possible to fall as quickly as it seemed Merced had? There was so much that she was unfamiliar with when it came to this kind of stuff.

She watched as his lashes fluttered and finally closed. She could feel the tension in his hand, the flex of his fingers but his touch remained a caress. It was so good, the taste, the feel, the eroticism of having him in her mouth. She licked and sucked and when she couldn't hold back she nipped at his cock with her teeth. And she hungered for more. She wanted his cock buried in her pussy. She wanted to ride him.

She wanted his kiss, the scrape of his tongue against hers. She wanted to run her tongue over his lips, to thrust her tongue between them and taste the flavour of his breath. Merced was slowly relaxing further beneath her so she kept sucking and working her hand up and down the shaft in rhythm with her mouth.

She slipped her free hand back between her thighs to play with her pussy. She stroked her finger back and forth over her clit and sucked his cock and the combination of the two had her quickly close to another orgasm. She just couldn't wait any longer, didn't care that he still wore the cloth on his hips. It didn't matter because the long thick stalk of his cock was free for her to take. That was just what she was going to do.

With a quick shift she pulled her mouth free and lifted to her knees over him. Luckily she had shifted while using her mouth so that she was astride him. That made it so much easier to lift and keeping him in her hand. She held him in place while she lowered onto him. The head nudged her opening and his eyes flared open wide. She thought he said no but she didn't give him time to stop her. With a hard downward thrust of her hips she buried half of his length inside her.

"Lynx," Merced groaned her name. She lifted her hips and slid down again taking more of him but still not managing to take every hard inch.

She let her eyes hold his and rose once more until just the head remained. She let her hands grip his chest and thrust down once more, harder and faster and took every inch inside her. Once more she felt like she was glowing, like every inch of her vibrated.

"Merced," she whispered and leaned into him. Her fingers gripped his shoulders and she let her nails dig deep as pleasure screamed through her. Leaning forward she found the corded muscle on one side of his neck and let her teeth grip him there, biting down. It was instinct for her. Her cat spirit was so close to the surface.

She heard his deep gasp for breath and immediately lifted from his neck to his mouth. Before he could stop her she locked her mouth to his open mouth and plunged her tongue deep. He was still, so still, and then with a shudder his breath slipped from his mouth to hers.

Her eyes flared. Her fingers clenched tight into his flesh and one part of her mind prayed she didn't break his skin. But the rest of her was locked into his gaze. As his breath filled her so did something else, everything else. Vaguely she could feel her pussy clenching and milking his cock, felt the spurt of his release as it filled her. But that was not what she focussed on. She was focussed on what filled her mind and when it finally eased she collapsed against Merced and wept.

Merced held his mate while she cried and wanted to die. He had let his guard down, let sensation overrule reason and now there would be little choice for his Lynx. They were completely linked now. The bond was formed between them. He had no idea how she would be though as he knew no Danuja that mated outside of their race. He was unsure how a shifter would deal with the bond that was formed, the link they would share.

"I'm so sorry, little cat," he told her as she continued to cry. "I should have stopped you."

She pulled away from him and though the tears still trailed down her cheeks her hand came out and smacked him hard on the chest. "If I had not done this then no one would probably have ever known all you suffered at his hands. You would have kept this from us all."

Merced didn't lie, it would do him no good anyway. So he just nodded his head. She smacked him again and then hugged him close. She shuddered against him and he held her close stroking his hand up and down her spine until she quieted. When she pulled away he didn't stop her but it was only to sit up beside him and talk.

"Is that what happened to you when I breathed into you?" she asked.

"Yes and no," he replied but continued before she could ask him to explain. "We were not intimately linked at the time so it was not as sharp for me."

"So because we were having sex it made it more intense for me?" she queried.

"Making love," he corrected. "And yes."

She smiled. "Making love," she agreed. "So you saw the same things about me?"

He smiled now. "Yes, I did. I saw everything from the moment you were born until the moment you breathed into me. You are a wild cat," he laughed.

"As you saw the things that I did with others then I will not comment on what I saw of you with others," she stated with a twinkle in her eyes and Merced could feel his skin flush red as he realised that she had indeed seen everything. "But seeing that and knowing that you saw the same in me explains a lot."

"Such as?" he asked.

"Why I was not kissed or made love to," she started to say but stopped.

"By my brother?" he finished for her and he couldn't stop the sadness that filled her, even though he knew she would feel it.

"I'm sorry," she whispered. "I didn't mean to hurt you."

"I know," he answered.

Her eyes searched his again. "I can feel your emotions. Is that part of this?" she asked and her hand moved back and forth between them.

"Yes," he whispered. "The bond is forming and will only grow stronger. We will feel each other's emotions. There will be no hiding from one another. It is the Danuja way."

"So no more lies or half truths," she smiled. "I kind of like that."

"It means the same for you," he reminded her but she didn't seem too concerned.

"You are aware of my feelings for Micah," she whispered. "I know that it hurts you and I would change that if I could. But there is just something there that I can't deny."

"I saw the night you shared with him," Merced whispered. "I know of your desire for the two of us, to share."

She smiled and there was no embarrassment in her. "Well you can't blame a girl for that," she said with a twinkle in her eyes. "He is your twin, the other half of you since birth. It only makes since that I would be attracted to him as well."

"And he healed you, leaving a piece of himself behind. He touched you, brought you to release," Merced smiled softly. "I would give you what you desire. He *is* my other half and though no Danuja has ever shared, for you, for him, I would."

"But he won't." It was a statement from her and he nodded.

"He is the holy man, the epitome of what is Danuja. He will not easily go against what we have been taught since birth," Merced said. His people would be shocked at what he was going to suggest but there was no hiding the secrets he kept inside from the woman he had mated. Honestly it was why he had not mated anyone before.

But Lynx didn't seem shocked or disgusted by the man he was. She smiled at him waiting to hear what he was going to say. With the sharing of his breath she had been witness to every moment of his life, even those he had hidden from everyone else. She had seen the sex he had shared with others, knew that he enjoyed sharing a woman. Just as he had seen the same desire in her. He had known since she breathed into him that she wanted both him and Micah. That was most of the reason he had held back from her. Micah might never accept a threesome.

No, his little cat had seen her sister Aurora happily mated to two men. Lynx saw her sister's joy and contentment and longed for the same. Merced would love to give it to her. As king none would question what he did, though they might discuss it behind his back. Micah was a different story. They would not be so easy on the holy man. But then neither he nor Micah had ever wanted the fate they had been born into. It was why Merced had been the one to play messenger and probably why Micah had been the brother to follow him. They longed for more, for adventure, for freedom from the confines of 'being Danuja royalty'.

The difference was that Merced had already admitted it to himself. Micah might never do that. Merced didn't know for sure what Micah had undergone when he had been separated from the family and taken to the temple for several years. The man who had returned had not been the same carefree person, and his power had changed as well. But Merced knew his brother, his twin. He could see the longing in Micah's eyes for a freedom they had never known.

Lynx knew his emotions but not his thoughts. She could sense what he felt just as he now could with her.

"What is it that you are planning, Merced?" she asked.

"I'll tell you in just a bit," he promised. "There is something else I want to do first."

She smiled and lay back on the bed spreading her legs as he shifted between them. "What is it you want to do?" she asked with that grin still in place.

"I want to love you until neither of us can move," he whispered leaning down so that his face was even with hers. "I want to kiss you without fear."

She hooked one arm behind his neck and lifted up to him. "Then kiss me, Merced. Kiss me until neither of us can breathe."

That was just what he intended to do.

Chapter Six

It was soft and sweet and everything she had dreamed of. She loved him and knew that he loved her. There was no way that she couldn't after she had witnessed every moment, every emotion of his life. Inside her heart still broke for what he worked so hard to deny himself, for the responsibilities he carried. She shuddered at the depths of the torture he had endured at Wilhelm's hands and wanted to kill the man a million times over.

"Shhhhh," Merced whispered to her as he pulled slowly from her lips. "No anger here, in this bed, in this moment. Only us," he said and bent to her lips once more. "Vengeance has no place here."

She nodded and did her best to shove her thoughts away and focus only on him, on them and the moment that existed right now. His hands were everywhere on her flesh, sparks left a trail from his fingertips and now she knew that she really was glowing with a golden shade. It was his magic flowing from his skin to hers. He couldn't control it with her and that thrilled her.

He smiled as he trailed his finger over her nipple and the spark lingered on that sensitive spot. Lynx arched and moaned, her fingers curling into the bed. The finger moved to the other nipple and treated it to the same torture.

"Merced," she moaned his name and he laughed. It was one of the most wondrous sounds she'd ever heard.

He leant over her and took one nipple into his mouth and sucked deeply. The magical ripple was replaced by a pinch and tug. Her hands reached for him, one bracing on his shoulder and the other going around to the back of his head to hold him to her. He slowly pulled back letting her nipple pop free. She moaned and he smiled.

"I love you, little cat," he whispered. "You are the most amazing woman I've ever known."

And she knew he meant it, could feel the emotion behind the words. No one, not her mother, her sister, or any shifter she'd been friends with knew her to the depth that her mate did. Her mate. It was bizarre and crazy and yet impossibly right. She loved him too. There was no way that she could not after what had passed between them.

He lifted his head and brought it to her. She smiled as their mouths met, meshed and loved.

He moved over her, wedged his body between her thighs and never once pulled from their kiss. They were already making love with his cock hard against her leg. With their mouths, their minds, their very souls. The body was only a part of the circle they created.

When he lifted from her his mouth moved to her jaw and up to her ear. He whispered and the words were of love no matter that he spoke in his native tongue. His cock probed her wet entrance and slowly slid deep. She lifted her knees to clamp at his hips. One hand went to the small of his back while the other caressed through his hair.

She loved the way he wore it long, the fat braids so different. She loved the darkness of his skin against her own, a deep brown. He wasn't as dark as Domi, her sister's mate who kept the black skin of his panther while in human form. Merced and his brother were a creamy version of that, a lovely brown that made her think of the rich fertile soil. His eyes were a deep gold the brown specs all but gone in his passion. His eyes made her think of the lion, whose form she loved to take.

Slow and easy he pumped inside her, his mouth constantly returning to sip from hers. She could feel the glow of his magic around them both. Lynx marvelled that even with the damper Wilhelm still held over Merced's magic he was still the most powerful man she'd ever met. The man possessed the power to do things she'd never imagined, never even thought of controlling.

Their eyes met and held. His mouth hovered just over hers and his breath washed across her. She could feel how much it meant to him to not have to control that little thing that she had never worried about. Yet he had always had to control that simple act. Never had he breathed into another, kissed another. It made her regret the fact that she had. She'd just never realised the true intimacy of a kiss.

One hand moved down between their bodies and she felt the spark directly on her clit.

"Merced," she cried out feeling her orgasm building. He was right with her, enjoying the build with her.

He quickened his thrusts, his cock moving faster, surging deeper within her. She met him thrust for thrust using her grip on his hips to help her lift into every downward stroke. One more pulse to her clit and she was flying through the air. Her head was thrown back, an unvoiced cry trapped on her lips.

She could feel his orgasm. Not only the pulse of his semen in her pussy but even better she could feel how his orgasm felt to him. She felt his pleasure just as she knew he felt hers and it took the intimacy to an entire different level. She remembered how not so long ago she had longed for what her sister Aurora shared with Domi and Nado. Now she couldn't imagine having anything different than what she shared with Merced. Only one thing would make it better.

Merced moved to lie beside her on the bed. "Now we plot," he said and Lynx laughed. The only thing that could possibly make things more perfect for her and Merced would be to include Micah. He was Merced's twin, the other part of her mate and important to them both. She did not have Micah's memories yet, nor his emotions, but she had Merced's of Micah. Through Merced she felt her feelings for Micah grow. She was in love with Merced and through him she loved Micah.

"Micah will never agree to join with us," Merced stated, relaxed beside her. She rested her head on his chest and loved the way it was just such a natural thing to do. One big hand stroked up and down her arm while the other ran through her hair. "It is against our culture to take more than one mate. Danuja mate for life and some would say even in death. No Danuja marries after their mate dies. It is as if through our link we die with one another as well."

"I can only imagine," Lynx whispered. "Having seen what you went through at Wilhelm's hands devastates me as if I felt it as well."

"You must let it go, little cat, and move on," Merced stated. "Vengeance will have its time, its place. But not at this moment."

"How do you do that?" she asked. "Just push things to the side."

"Years of practice," he sighed and she thought of the burden that came with the title he held. It made her think of Aslan, her king, the twin of the woman she had always thought of as her sister, in a new light. There was much that rested on the shoulders of a king.

"There are two things that work in our favour when it comes to my brother," Merced continued, his arms back to stroking her. "One is the simple fact that he is my twin, my other half. In my culture many say that twins are one soul split into two people. So it is not uncommon for only one of the two to mate while the other seemingly remains alone. Now I wonder if there is not more to that than we have been aware of. The Danuja are a mystical people and secrets are easy to keep from one another. We do not share our kiss, our breath, our souls easily and so when we do, it is forever."

"And I took that choice from you when I breathed into you," Lynx whispered. She knew he loved her but had to wonder if it was because of the link they shared, the one her act of ignorance had brought upon them.

"And I thank you for that," he whispered bending to brush her lips with his. "It is a choice I would have wished for and yet felt compelled to walk away from. I would choose to walk away instead of sharing my life, my emotional self with another. And I yearned for you even when you came to me as a small cat."

Lynx laughed as she knew he intended her to. "I did not know what that moment would bring us to and would have found another means at the time to revive you had I been aware. Much for the same reason I suppose. I would not wish to bind a mate to me fearing the vulnerability it would bring. Yet, I wouldn't change it for anything now. Lying here in this bed with you is the most perfect moment of my life." She cupped his face feeling his emotion in tandem with hers. "And I can only imagine it getting better."

"And that brings me to the other thing that works in our favour," Merced offered.

"What is that?" she asked.

"You," he whispered and they began to plot.

Micah felt as if his soul was ripped from his body as he shut the door and walked away. She was the one, the only one. Lynx should have shared his breath, his soul, his life. He could still taste her on his tongue, feel the smooth skin of her pussy under his tongue. And now she was forbidden. Danuja mated for life. Lynx was his brother's mate.

It didn't matter what wishes had filled his head, his heart. It only mattered what was. He made it down the hall, down the stairs and outside the walls that felt as if they were closing in on him. He had never felt less holy in his life. He would give almost anything to shirk the cloak of being the Damisau of his people.

He didn't know how long he had walked nor how far when he heard the sighs and moans on the breeze. It appeared he'd stumbled upon the love play of the queen Aurora and her mates Domi and Nado. The three were entwined with one man under her while the other embraced her from behind.

As a holy man he should have been repulsed. As a Danuja he should have immediately turned and walked away. As a man he stood routed to the spot and wished that it was Merced on that ground with Lynx. And Micah wished with all he was that he was the man with them.

Finally he turned and walked away heading deeper into the wood. He needed solitude, time to commune and renew his spirit. He was lost in his thoughts, immune to what was happening around him. He never saw the men who stepped out of the shadows and followed him. When the blow caught him on the base of his skull he fell easily and for the moment his thoughts did not torture him.

The two men struggled to haul the dead weight of the big Danuja on the unmarked trail that led to one of their scattered camps. They would be highly rewarded for their capture. They would have all they wanted. They would live like kings when Wilhelm saw the bounty they brought. He wanted the big Danuja badly. And luck was with them as Wilhelm was there when the dragged the body in.

"You have him," Wilhelm demanded immediately heading towards them. He gripped the thick braids and lifted the head to his line of vision. "You idiots!" He screamed at them. "Fools, you've grabbed the wrong man. There are only two of them and yet still you manage to screw it up."

"He fell into our hands, my lord," one of them pleaded knowing that their lives depended on how Wilhelm reacted.

"You dragged him all the way here," Wilhelm shook his head and it was easy to see the disgust on his face. "You left a trail all the way here. So take your sorry asses back out there and figure out a way to remove that trail."

Both of the men jumped to follow that order.

Wilhelm watched them leave and turned to the remaining men in the camp. "You will need to pick up and move to another location. Make sure it is as secure as this one once was."

"The two you sent out?"

At the question Wilhelm turned to one of the men who captained his dwindling ranks. "Find them and kill them."

The man merely nodded. "And the Danuja?"

Wilhelm looked down at the man before him. His restrained power would not be useful to Wilhelm. No it was the other Danuja's he craved as his own.

"Kill him."

Chapter Seven

Lynx still couldn't find Micah and now she had lost track of Merced as well. This mate thing was going to drive her crazy. Especially since she could feel Merced's growing worry. Her mate couldn't hide it from her and it increased her worry as well. She was just turning a corner when she ran into her sister Aurora coming out of a room.

"Have you seen Micah?" Lynx asked.

"Not recently," Aurora answered. "Have a minute?"

"Sure," Lynx smiled as Aurora grabbed her hand and squeezed before leading her into the room she'd just walked out of.

"Sit with me for a minute," Aurora said and pointed to two chairs. "So much has happened in so short a time. I want to make sure that you are okay."

"Of course I am," Lynx automatically stated and her sister shook her head.

"This is me you are talking to," Aurora stated.

Lynx took a deep breath. "I always knew that you weren't really my sister but there was always this connection between us. I know that you are queen and I can't tell you how proud I am of you. You will be an amazing queen. I'm also happy that you have found your family, your brother, your home. I know how much you wondered where you came from." Lynx laughed. "Do you remember the stories we used to create and act out?" Aurora joined in and it was good to see her laugh. "I just want you to know that I'm always here for you. I know that you have Aslan and it is important to explore your relationship with him. He is your twin after all. Just remember that I love you and always have."

Aurora leaned in and hugged Lynx to her. "And you remember that I will always love you. Our bond is stronger than blood. You are the sister of my heart and nothing can change that." Aurora pulled back but stayed close. "I would love for you to stay here with me, to be a part of everything I hope to do."

Lynx smiled and shook her head. "My life is changing also and I can't promise that I will remain here. But I can promise that I will always return when you need me."

"Micah?" Aurora asked softly and Lynx wanted to laugh and cry at the same time.

"It is a long story," Lynx sighed. "One that is not finished playing out just yet."

"You will tell me when the time is right?" Aurora asked and Lynx loved that her sister didn't pry.

"Yes," she vowed. "Now I have to find Micah and Merced."

"Merced was with Aslan earlier discussing some things," Aurora stated. "Which reminds me, Lake and Lincoln left this morning for the camp. Mamma should be here in a few days."

Lynx caught her breath. The danger her mother could face scared the hell out of her. She would give anything to keep Lydia safely hidden from Wilhelm's eyes. But then was that even possible? Another part of her was happy her mother was coming. She wanted to share the fact that she was now mated with her as well as whom she was mated to. She had no doubt that once her mother saw how happy she was, how much she felt for Merced and hopefully Micah, Lydia would be happy as well.

"We will watch over and keep her safe," Aurora vowed.

"Yes," Lynx agreed. There was so much she needed to tell Aurora but she could feel Merced's anxiety growing it was hard to sit still. "I have to go for now. I really need to find Micah and Merced."

Aurora gave her a funny look, then looked closer at her. Finally a smile crossed her lips and Lynx knew that her sister was aware of the sexual glow she wore. Lynx could feel the skin of her face flushing bright red.

"So that is the way of it," Aurora said. "I wish the three of you all the love my mates and I share."

"Only two of us at the moment," Lynx muttered and Aurora laughed.

"Merced or Micah?" Aurora asked.

"Merced," Lynx answered shaking her head at the look of surprise on her sister's face. "There is so much about the Danuja culture that I am still learning. So much I need talk to you about." Like the fact that Lynx was a queen now as well. "But I really need to find them now."

"I understand," Aurora said. "I will help you look." They both rose and hugged once more. "When the time is right I will be here to listen."

Lynx nodded and felt some of her tension leave. She had been worried that things might change and be different with Aurora now. But her sister was still her sister and it didn't seem like that was in danger of changing. They stepped out into the hallway.

"I'll head out and see if Domi or Nado have seen either of them," Aurora said, giving her hands another squeeze.

"Thanks," Lynx said. "If you see them let them know that I am looking for them."

Aurora nodded and turned to walk away. Lynx turned and went the other way down the hall. The castle home of Aslan and now Aurora and her mates was huge. It would take forever to search the structure. She turned towards the stairs and Aslan was coming up them.

"A moment, Lynx?" he asked.

Especially if she kept getting stopped for conversation she thought with a sigh. "Sure," Lynx said. "Have you seen Merced?"

Aslan sighed and she could see the worry on his face, the stress he was weighted under. "Yes," he murmured. "We spoke briefly and made plans to assemble the group and speak more in depth in a few hours. There are things that he can tell us, things that we must know in order to defeat Wilhelm."

"I'm sorry," Lynx whispered and reached out to him giving his arm a firm squeeze. "I can't imagine what you must be going through. I would wish that none of this had happened but then I would not have been blessed with my sister."

"You love her very much," he smiled at Lynx. "And I am learning that not everything that I was taught is true." He seemed lost in thought for just a moment but then focused on her again. "I want you to know that I think of you as my sister as well. It is hard not to when my twin sister loves you so much. You will always have a home here with us and I would be honoured if you would think of me as a brother."

Lynx just nodded. She wasn't sure that she would be able to think of him as a brother, but she would see him as a friend. "Thank you."

"Before you go I want to let you know that Lake and Lincoln are leaving today to head to your village and bring your mother safely to us. They will guard and protect her with their lives," Aslan stated quietly.

Lynx nodded. "Aurora just told me."

"I also want you to know that she will be respected and honoured by me. I realise that what was told me as truth is not. I pray that your mother can shed more light on what happened long ago. On my mother and her death." He looked so sad for a moment and without thought Lynx stepped close and hugged him.

"We will find the truth among the lies," she vowed.

He hugged her a moment and then released her. "Yes, we will," he agreed.

"Did Merced say where he was headed?" she queried.

"The courtyard outside, I believe," Aslan stated and was interrupted by an earth shaking roar.

"Merced," Lynx yelled and took off at a run. Something was wrong. Something was very wrong. She knew it had something to do with Micah and could not get to Merced fast enough. Vaguely she saw that Aslan followed closely behind her. When they burst outside Merced was standing and there was a wide circle around him as if none felt comfortable enough to approach him. It could have been the rage in his eyes, the quiver of his massive body. More than likely it was the magic that crackled in the air surrounding him.

Aurora was there with her mates Domi and Nado. She saw Piers and Seer there as well but she really only had eyes for Merced. She stepped right into his magic and his arms automatically opened to pull her close.

"What happened?" she demanded.

"It is Micah," he whispered but she knew everyone could hear him. "He is unconscious. I fear that something has happened to him."

"Is he alive?" she whispered feeling Merced's fear as her own.

"His life force is still intact," Merced replied. "But if he was taken there is only one who would want him."

"Wilhelm," she breathed.

"Wilhelm," Merced agreed. "We must hurry and find him."

"The woods are immense around the keep," Aslan said. "I will have my men set up search parties immediately."

"Forgive me if I don't place my brother's life in the hands of your men," Merced sneered and Lynx tensed.

But Aslan just hung his head with resignation and finally nodded. "I understand. But I will lead one of the groups myself and Piers and Seer will lead as well. We know this area, where the hidden dangers might lie."

Merced nodded and Lynx moved to stand by her mate's side though he linked his hand with hers to keep their flesh bond. "I did not mean to imply that I could not trust you," he stated to Aslan. "But I have been at Wilhelm's mercy for too long to trust easily."

"Understood," Aslan answered. "I will go with you then, we will cover more ground if we split up. Aurora can go with Piers and Seer. I figure Domi, Nado, and Lynx will want to shift and go on their own." He turned to address the guys but also glanced at Lynx to include her. "You will know the dangers better in your cat forms than probably even I. Stay on guard and let out a roar if you find him." He turned to Piers and Seer then. "I will take my horn and you both do the same. Use it to call if you come across him. We must hurry and pray for the best."

Lynx turned to Merced. "We will find him. We must."

"I pray you are right, little cat," Merced said and hugged her close once more. She barely came to his chest and it made her feel small and dainty. He bent and she lifted and their lips fused. She could feel his magic wrapping around her holding them both. So much power lay within Merced. More than anyone could imagine. He broke the kiss and looked deeply into her eyes unaware or uncaring of the enraptured gazes of their audience. "Be safe for my heart and soul travel with you."

"And mine with you," she replied before easing from him. They had to get moving for neither of them would be whole if something happened to Micah.

They finally separated and when she turned it was easy to see the questions in the eyes of everyone but her sister. Thanks to their talk earlier, her sister knew a little about her and Merced.

"Let's go," she stated, moving towards Domi and Nado.

"We'll head to the right," Aslan stated. "Aurora, you and Piers and Seer go to the left. Lynx, Domi and Nado go right up the middle. And everyone remember to sound off if you spot him."

They all nodded and turned away. Lynx was already shifting and when she hit the ground it was as the wild tiger. Best for battle and great for tracking. And it didn't hurt that she had two panthers with her.

They were faster than the others, not having to depend on a mount to get them around. Domi and Nado stayed right with her as she took off at a run. She prayed that Micah was okay.

After sending a small group of men after the two idiot soldiers, the captain watched Wilhelm head out. He glanced down at the now bound and gagged unconscious

Danuja with disgust. "Clean the camp up as quickly as you can," he ordered.

"What about him?" one of the men motioned towards the bound prisoner.

The captain hit the man so hard that he fell to the ground. "Do what I said and don't ask stupid questions. You heard Wilhelm. When we are ready to go we will kill him."

Micah laid there pretending to still be unconscious. The back of his head throbbed where they had used something to knock him out. His hands and feet were bound once more and this time he was gagged as well. There was only one thing that made this time different from the first time Wilhelm's men had captured him. This time he no longer cared if he lived or died. In many ways he thought it might actually be better if he were to just disappear without a trace.

He saw once more the developing bond between Lynx and Merced and felt the stab of jealousy deep inside. It was not right for a holy man to feel such evil emotion. It was a sin to lust after another's mate, especially his twin's. And if he were around he always would. He would never be able to look at Lynx without remembering the taste of her on his tongue, the sound of her pleasure, the feel of her skin. He would always lust… No, love what was not his to love. And every day he would slowly die a little more anyway.

He stole a look at the camp from beneath his lashes and noticed that they were close to being packed up and ready to travel. He could see the wicked blades strapped to their sides and wondered briefly if they would torture before they killed. Tied as he was he would be unable to defend himself even if he wanted to. A picture of Lynx entered his mind and he swore he could hear her laughter on the breeze.

His heart was heavy. So with deep concentration he took himself under to the place within that would shield and allow healing. Or in this case allow him to die without once begging for mercy. No matter what they did.

Chapter Eight

Lynx measured her pace as they entered the woods, knowing that it was important to slow down and let her senses feel what was around her. She could not run blindly through or she might miss something that would point her in the right direction. Domi and Nado eased their pace as well and they spread out a bit allowing them to cover a wider range of area. Lynx stayed in the middle of them and deliberately began to search for the scent she needed to find.

The woods were thick with trees and bushes, the ground covered in vines and thick grasses. Wildlife thrived there and she could feel the natural instinct of the animal form she was in wanting to hunt for prey. With this so close to the keep she knew that Domi and Nado would be content in their new home. They could easily run here and feed the souls of the panthers within them.

They hadn't gone far when she came across the first human scent. Within a few more feet it was stronger.

Someone had been through here recently. The grass was trampled in a smooth path indicating that whoever it was had been trying to remain hidden. Lynx stopped and let the scent fill her senses. Slowly she crept forward following the same path. There had been two men at this point and she could scent them both.

As she moved forward another scent caught her nostrils, one that she was more than familiar with. Micah. He had been here and the two scents she had already picked up on had snuck up on him. She wanted to run but eased forward instead locking on Micah's scent, which seemed to be getting stronger. As she stepped into the middle of the clearing she knew why. Blood. A small trail of it leading away where something or someone had been dragged.

Micah. That was why his scent was so strong. That was his blood. She threw back her massive tiger head and let loose a mighty roar that echoed through the forest. Domi and Nado quickly rejoined her and they all shifted back to human form.

"I was already heading your way," Domi said. "I picked up Micah's scent and was following it back this way."

"The same for me," Nado replied. "Only the scent I found was not Micah's. There were two scents and they had moved this way."

"They must have met up with him here," Lynx stated pointing to the ground.

Domi squatted down. "Blood," he stated looking up at Lynx.

"Micah's," she whispered.

"They dragged him out of here," Nado stated, looking at the clear path leading away. "It will be easy to follow them from this point." Lynx was ready her very cells vibrating with the need to shift and run, but Nado stopped her with a hand on her shoulder. "We do not know what we head into, so remain cautious and do not let your emotion control you."

"Was it easy for you to do when it was Aurora we searched for?" she replied.

"Just stay safe, Sister," Domi said from her other side. "It would kill Aurora if anything happened to you."

Lynx nodded taking a deep breath. "Let's go," she said, feeling a pull to hurry and find Micah.

Domi cocked his head when the sound of horns filled the air. "They heard your cry and are heading our way."

"I won't wait for them," she said.

Nado nodded in agreement. "Neither will we."

Together they shifted once more and walked the path left for them. The blood was spotty, indicating that it wasn't a rapidly bleeding wound. She had to pray that was good and that Micah was okay. She could sense worry the closer Merced got to her but no sense of loss as if Micah were already gone.

As they moved the scent of fresh blood caught her nostrils and she wanted to surge forward at a fast run. But as the scent grew she realised that it wasn't Micah's. It was different and yet the same. It was that of the other two and it was fresher and stronger. When she came upon the site it was easy to see why.

The two men lay in a pool of blood. Both had been stabbed. The first had been caught by surprise and taken out easily. One stab wound straight to the heart was all he had. The other had put up a fight. He had multiple wounds on his hands, arms and torso. But finally he must have tired and he too had a wound over his heart. She felt no pity for them, no remorse for the loss of their lives. They had to be the ones who had spilled Micah's blood so this death was much easier than the one she would have given.

With Domi and Nado inches behind her she followed another trail, a newer one that the killers had left in their hurry. No stealth or attempt to cover their tracks here. Just a kill and flee. She quickened her pace and hurried to follow. If they would kill their own then what would they do to Micah? She remembered hearing that when he was captured by Wilhelm and in the wagon with Aurora that he was to be burned alive. She didn't smell smoke as of yet but that was no guarantee.

She let out another mighty roar as they burst into a clearing that must have once been a camp. Micah lay prone on the ground with blood around him. He had been beaten and if not for his clothes and size she might not have recognised him. She let out another roar this one filled with the fear and anguish coursing through her and shifted by his side.

Falling to her knees she reached for him, afraid to touch and yet unable to not. "Micah," she whispered. "Micah, what have they done to you?" His pulse was weak, his heart barely beating and there seemed to be no breath in his body.

Without thought she did the same as she had done to Merced. She leaned in and pinching his nose tilted his face back. Tipping his chin down with one finger she opened his mouth and locked hers to it. And breathed into him. She knew the ramifications this time, knew how it would connect them if he made it through. It didn't matter. It was what she and Merced wanted anyway. Merced had told her that the only way was for her to bond with Micah, but neither of them had wanted it to be this way.

She breathed into him again and again not willing to stop until he opened his eyes. "Don't you dare die on me

Micah. Don't you dare," she implored feeling the tears running down her cheeks. "I need you. Merced needs you. Our lives won't be complete without you. You have to fight for us, for all of us."

"Lynx," he whispered her name and her eyes flew up to lock on his. His sweet golden eyes were dark amber and filled with pain. "Too late," he rasped. "Damage inside," he managed and she could hear the labour of his voice and knew what it cost him to speak to her.

"Hold on for me," she pleaded. "Don't give up."

"Kiss me," he whispered. "Kiss me just once."

She leaned down to him and pressed their lips together once more. This time she let her tongue slip inside, felt the rub of his against it and was invaded by the rush of his memories, his pain, and knew that no matter the outcome the men who had done this to him would die. After she was finished punishing them.

She sucked his tongue, ate at Micah's mouth and enjoyed the feel of it, of him. She could feel the beginning of the bond between them and didn't want to let go. It was Micah who turned his mouth to gasp for air. She followed the line of his jaw to his neck and up to his ear licking, sucking and nipping with her teeth.

"Love you," he whispered and he sounded weaker. "Was never anyone before you and would never have been another after you."

"Don't speak like that Micah," she implored. "Merced is on his way. We are bonded now. Me to both of you. You can't leave me. You can't."

"Will never leave you," he promised and his eyes drifted closed. The slowing pulse stopped and having made the bond Lynx could feel Micah slipping away for good.

A roar rumbled through the earth beneath them. The wind whipped through the trees. Thunder boomed in the sky overhead though no storm existed. And Merced burst through the trees on horseback. A fierce cry echoed around them as he jumped from the mount and moved towards them. Fire was in his eyes, flames at his fingertips and each step brought another tremble from the ground, another boom from the sky above.

She could feel the emotions flowing through him. Anger, pain, fear, and the certainty that he could bring Micah back.

"Together," he said kneeling on the other side of Micah. "To forge the bond so that none of our people can question we must do this together." He took her hands and placed them on the centre of Micah's chest and placed his over the top of them. "No matter what, do not move your hands."

She felt the heat first, a warmth that slipped from Merced, through her and into Micah. Slow and steady at first it grew hotter and coursed faster. A glow began around them as if shielding them while Merced worked to heal.

"What!" Merced exclaimed and his face took on a fierce expression as he must have felt something. When she looked at him in question he simply said, "A barrier lies within him, confining his power, powers I did not even realise we shared."

Merced closed his eyes and the fiery heat burned hotter and she looked at her hands just to reassure herself that they did not burn. Instinct had her wanting to pull them free but love kept them firmly planted between the two men.

She could feel the push of power from Merced growing stronger as he worked on the barrier that Micah had within him. She knew what it was from and soon Merced would as well. She had only to focus on what she had seen in Micah's memory for Merced to know what was done to his brother when he was sent to the temple to be trained as a holy man. They had tortured him, bound the majority of his powers and vowed him to silence about it all. Only his mate would be able to fully understand what he had gone through, and rarely did the holy man mate.

Merced gave a fierce cry and she felt the crack of the binding and the unbearable hit quickly moved through her and filled Micah. Merced began to chant and though she did not know the language she understood what he was saying. He was calling the soul back while the heat of his magic healed and refreshed Micah's flesh. She prayed to the goddess begging her to restore Micah, to not take him from her.

Time seemed to stand still. Moments lasted a lifetime before Micah finally blinked his eyes open. With a cry she leant down to him smothering his beautiful face with kisses. No visible marks of the beating he had taken remained. Merced had healed them all.

Micah smiled and caught her lips with his, plundering her mouth with a kiss that seared hotter than the magical flames. It left her panting for breath, panting for more, much more.

"You brought me back," he said and his eyes were on Merced.

"I could not let my twin die while I had life left in me," Merced stated.

"We are bound now," Micah said and Merced nodded.

"We are all bound now," Merced agreed. "Mated for life."

"And you would share so great a gift with me?" Micah whispered.

"I would die for you," Merced stated.

"Brother," Micah said and lifted his hand to Merced. Merced linked his with it and pulled it to hold their joined hands over his heart.

"From this day forward we walk together," Merced said. "No king, no holy man, only brothers joined by heart, by soul, and by the love of the one mate they share. Had I but known of the binding they placed on you I would have removed it long ago. Your powers are yours, given unto you at birth and none should ever be allowed to take those gifts from you. Never."

"It is the way of the holy man," Micah said as he sat up pulling Lynx over into his lap and holding her close. "Generations before me have known the same."

"Never again will a Danuja be subjected to that," Merced vowed. "Not while we are king."

"We?" Micah asked with a smile.

"It is as it should have always been," Merced nodded. "Twins should not be separated. Two halves of one soul can only truly be whole when together. Our people will learn to accept that."

"And the fact that we share one mate between us?" Micah asked, looking at Lynx.

"They will accept or they will be free to leave," Merced stated. "I feel that the people are more than ready for change to come. Only the elder generation will hold true to the old ways, and yet, I feel that even many of them will come around when they see the joy we share."

Micah nodded and bent to kiss Lynx once more. She felt it all the way to her toes. She wanted to strip right there and mate fully with Micah no matter the audience they still held.

"Aurora will be pleased that you follow in her footsteps," Domi's voice cut in.

"What?" she asked.

"If Merced and Micah are kings and you are mated to them, then that would make you a queen," Nado said with a laugh.

"Just as your sister," Domi added laughing as well.

Lynx just shook her head and grinned. At least Domi and Nado seemed okay with the fact that she was mated to two men. Then why wouldn't they when they were both mated to the same woman?

"Let's head back," Micah said and wrapping one hand under her hips used the other to push himself up and stand.

She wrapped her arms tight around his neck and held tight. "Are you okay to leave?"

His golden eyes smouldered and she could feel the sexual need surrounding him, surrounding them. "I am more than ready to head back," was his husky reply.

"You two head back," Merced said.

"What about you?" Lynx asked not liking the idea of Merced going off without them.

"I intend to see what else we can find," Merced said and kept going before either she or Micah could interrupt with their displeasure. "I have two panthers and a king with me and the queen and her warriors should be here soon." He moved to them and kissed her softly on the mouth before whispering to her. "You and Micah need this time to fully join. He deserves no less than what we shared. And when I return we can show what it is to have two men worship you."

"No risks, Merced," she whispered back.

"No risks," he promised and kissed her once more, his tongue filling her mouth and saturating her veins with pleasure.

"Take my mount," he told Micah and took her into his arms while Micah mounted the horse. Merced handed her up to his brother and she sat across the front of Micah's lap her arms wrapping around his neck once more and holding tight.

The brothers shared a look and she could feel the love and acceptance pass between them. Micah would not fight Merced against being in this relationship with them. With the breaking of the barrier that had confined him it was as if he was a different person. And she thanked the goddess for giving him back to them.

She snuggled against him wiggling on the erection under her bottom. He groaned and urged the horse faster. She was just as anxious to get back and mate completely with Micah. Having tasted his kiss, and recalling the one night they had shared, she was eager to make love with him. And in mere moments she would.

Chapter Nine

Micah shut the door behind them and just leant back and looked at Lynx.

"What?" she asked afraid that maybe he had changed his mind, maybe he did not want her or to share her with Merced. So much was floating through her head.

But he only smiled. "You are the most beautiful woman I have ever seen. I can't believe that in just moments I will be able to touch you, all of you with no fear."

She grinned and reached for the hem of her shirt tugging it up and over her head. His breath caught at the sight of her naked breasts and it made her feel beautiful, powerful. She moved to sit on the edge of the bed and slowly removed her shoes before standing once more and reaching for the laces of her leathers. She slid them down her hips and kicked them aside before looking up and staring into his face.

His gaze was eating her as it raked from head to toe and back again. She could tell how much he desired her by the level of heat in his eyes. They smouldered like molten gold and she could feel herself falling into them. He eased away from the door and reached inside his robe as he moved towards her. It hit the floor at their feet leaving him in the snug fabric she had first discovered on Merced. She was really beginning to like them.

His cock was long and thick with hunger, and before he could do anything she dropped to her knees in front of him. It only took a moment to reach up and tug him free of the material. His cock bobbed in front of her, the tip glistening with the dampness of his desire. Leaning in she wrapped her lips around the head and sucked greedily at it.

He tasted like nothing she had ever known before. Wild and sweet and musky. Hot and hard and alive. His hips moved forward and more of his length pressed into the stretched confines of her mouth. He was incredibly delicious and she wanted more of his taste. She used one hand to wrap around the base of his shaft and the other to scrape her nails along the inside of his thigh. It seemed to drive him wild.

"Lynx," he moaned her name. "I want to love you, to touch and taste you."

She would have told him soon. She would have promised him later. But she would have had to stop sucking his cock long enough first and it wasn't happening. She looked up into his eyes instead and holding his gaze moved her mouth back and forth on him taking a little more of his length with every return. He groaned and sifted his fingers through her hair to caress her head.

He groaned again and began pumping his hips, fucking into her mouth. It was so good. She was blown away with how much she was enjoying having his cock in her mouth.

She rubbed her tongue in the groove just under the head and scraped her teeth there as well. Micah definitely liked that as his hips jerked thrusting him into the back of her throat. She gagged a little and he quickly pulled back and free.

"I'm sorry," he murmured as he pulled her to her feet.

"I wasn't finished," she tried to protest but he just shook his head.

"I need you," he whispered. "I want to be deep in your sweet pussy the first time I come."

"Yes," she moaned.

He turned her to face the bed and nudged her until she was bent over and with her ass in the air and her legs wide apart. She glanced over her shoulder at him and was seared by the heat of his gaze. It was his turn to fall to his knees and when he did it put his mouth even with her exposed cunt. He spread her lips and licked her from her clit all the way back to her ass. She cried out as he jabbed his tongue at her anus. It was different and incredible and scary all at the same time.

"I want to take you there," he whispered. "I want to feel the snug grip of your ass as I thrust inside you. Would you let me?"

"Yes," she whispered unwilling to deny him anything at the moment.

With a smile his face disappeared again between her spread thighs and his lips covered her clit. He sucked and licked the nub and two fingers pushed into her pussy. She gripped the bed with her fingers and held on as he took her closer and closer towards orgasm. Lips, tongue, teeth and fingers worked and every time she felt her juices spill he would take some on his fingers and move to her anus using her own wetness to lubricate there.

She came with a low moan and his fingers moved from her pussy only to be replaced by the thrusting of his tongue. His wet fingers moved back to her anus and this time one pushed inside past the first ring of muscle and kept going until she could feel the brush of his knuckles against her cheek. He thrust his tongue deep and held it still as well, then began moving in and out of her with both of them together.

She came again with a loud cry and found her body thrusting back on him wanting more. Words were spilling from her lips, begging for more, begging for him to fuck her. Micah rose to his feet behind her. One finger had become two and he moved them in and out of her anus slow and easy. It was a wicked burn followed by a searing tingle that connected to her nipples and clit and spiralled out further to the tips of her toes and fingers.

His cock nudged the opening of her pussy and when his fingers were just in, so that only the tips remained in her he paused. She glanced back at him over her shoulder and when their eyes connected he thrust deep. Fingers and cock slamming into her bringing a riot of satisfaction. She screamed and bucked taking him deeper in both places. The pleasure was so intense that it was painful. As if she were only moments away from exploding into a million pieces her body unable to contain the extreme emotion tearing through her.

"Micah," she cried his name out and he thrust a little faster, taking her a little harder, going deeper with every plunge.

His fingers were spearing inside her now shifting apart inside her to stretch her. He drove deep one more time and used his fingers to rub his cock through the thin barrier of tissue that separated him. Her nerve endings were already screaming and whether it was the feel of what he was doing or the knowledge she went hurtling over the edge into orgasm again. It ripped through her with a wave of cataclysmic bliss. Her body was lifted on her toes, her fingers clenched deep into the bed. Her head was thrown back and the cry she'd meant to scream was trapped in her throat.

It was too much to contain and her body was stretched taut as it surged through her. She held that way for what felt like moments and Micah stilled behind her letting her ride the wave without forcing more on her. Finally with a wail she collapsed down. Her feet flattened to the floor and her elbows hit the bed, her head dropping to rest between her spread arms. If not for his hand at her hip she probably would not have remained standing.

Micah slowly eased free of her and she realised that he was still rock hard. The fingers slipped from her ass and she felt the tuck of his cock at the opening. She might have tensed, might have let her nerves get to her but she was too sated, too limp from ecstasy for her body to listen. She realised that must have been what he had intended.

His cock was soaked in her juices and easily slipped inside the tight opening of her anus. She felt the tug and burn as he pressed past that first ring of muscle and then he slowly eased in until she could feel the brush of his sac against her ass cheeks. He held still allowing them both to adjust to the new sensations raging through them. Then when she couldn't help but wiggle just a bit, trying to adjust to the new feelings this brought her, he groaned and moved.

Both of his hands held her hips, keeping her lifted to his every glide in and out of her ass. Slow and easy he rode her and she could hear the pleasure it gave him in the way he whispered her name and how much he loved her. But even better, through their link she could feel how much he loved it, how much pleasure he found in her. Feeling his pleasure increased hers.

As his breath came faster so did his thrusts. Soon she was back up on her toes, fingers clenched once more and Micah pressed harder, faster and deeper with every plunge of his cock. She loved it, was already imagining how it would feel to have Micah taking her there while Merced was in her pussy. And goddess, she couldn't wait to find out.

Micah moved one hand around to her stomach and his fingers eased between her hips and the bed. He found her clit and began to rub across it moving back and forth as he thrust. In just seconds she was close to another orgasm. She rubbed herself on his fingers and then pushing back into his cock.

He was close. She could feel how close he was and on his next stroke she clenched around his shaft. With a cry he bucked, driving even deeper and held her hip as he spilled inside her. She could feel the heat of his seed washing inside her and came again coating his fingers where she rubbed against him.

She collapsed to the bed once more and he leaned over her gasping for breath as well. She turned her head to him and his lips found hers immediately. His kiss was soft, a reflection of the love in his eyes. She could taste herself on his lips. He eased back and she felt him move his hips so that he slowly slipped free of the tight grip of her anus. She groaned and shifted as her body felt the loss of his flesh.

Micah stood and bending lifted her up into his arms. He carried her to the top of the bed and bent over to lay her as close to the middle as he could before joining her there. He pulled a cover over them before taking her into his arms once more.

"I love you," she told him and felt tears prick her eyes and spill over. She did love him and today she could have lost him.

"Shhhh, my love," he whispered back reading her emotions and using his thumb to wipe her tears away. "I'm alive and well here in your arms."

He kissed her once more and lying in his arms she gave in to the sleep that wanted to pull her under. Micah was with her and Merced would join them soon. For the first time in a while she could really rest.

She awoke to the soft caresses of hands stroking over her skin. Four hands. One set was stroking her right side while the other focused on her left. Starting at her shoulders they moved slowly down her body brushing over her rock hard nipples before trailing over her hips. She moaned and shifted.

"I was hoping you would awaken sooner," Merced stated from her left.

She took in the sight of him. Clothed he was a beautiful man but naked he was unbelievable. His body was pure perfection. His chest was sprinkled with coarse hair that twined into a path that led to his stomach and then lower to the jutting length of his cock. He was hard and hungry for her. She licked her lips and he groaned.

Micah chose that moment to pinch her nipple dragging a gasp from her and turning her head his way. He was just as deliciously naked as Merced and just as thick with hunger. She slipped down the bed so that her hands would reach their cocks and gripped them in her hands giving them a squeeze. Both of her men groaned.

She smiled. This is what she had envisioned from the beginning. This is what she had wanted, the three of them together. She made love with Merced and then with Micah and now, finally, the three of them would be together.

"Tell me this is not a dream," she murmured. "That you are both here and that we will all be together."

"No dream, little cat," Merced whispered then moaned as she moved her hand along his length.

"We are all together," Micah agreed offering a groan of pleasure as she stroked him as well.

"Are you okay with this, Micah?" she asked, knowing that he felt the biggest burden among them. He was the one who had been taken and raised in the ways of the holy men of the Danuja. He was the one that she worried would feel pressured to leave her and Merced.

"No worry or fear here," Micah said. "When Merced placed his hands on me, over yours. When you brought me back. The restraints were removed and I am finding that my thinking is no longer clouded by thoughts of generations before me. I feel free for the first time since I was a child. Free to love as I see fit, as I desire."

"And when the time comes for us to return?" Lynx asked needing to know that things would not change when they went to the Danuja lands.

"Micah and I have much to discuss," Merced stated. "But I think we both would rather stay here with you."

"But you are king," she exclaimed squeezing their cocks in her agitation and bringing pleasurable hisses as they gritted their teeth and arched up into her touch. "And Micah is still the holy man as far as they are concerned."

"We will have to return," Micah stated moving her hand from his cock and taking it between both of his. "But we do not have to stay. We want for you to meet our family, our mother, brothers, and sisters. But though it is the life we were born into, it is not the one either of us would have chosen."

"And yet sometimes we must do what is expected of us," Lynx stated, she moved her other hand from Micah's cock to his shoulder and turned her head back and forth between them. "You are the powers that be for your people. I'm sure they must trust and love you. Don't make any decisions yet, especially not on my account. Once we have dealt with Wilhelm and things are settled here we can head to your home and see what the feeling is when we are there."

"You would leave your home for us?" Micah asked.

"I know that you can feel my emotions," Lynx stated. "So I won't tell you that I'm not feeling anxious about going there. I am mated to the king and their holy man. We are a triad though that is not your custom. So, yes, it makes me nervous. But I love you both. Feeling the way you feel for me there is no way that I could not. So I will go where you need me to. As long as I am free to shift and be myself then there is no fear within me."

"We would have you no other way," Merced swore.

"Then let's make no decisions until we return and see for ourselves the reception," she said. "People have a way of surprising you."

The brothers exchanged a look and then both nodded. Merced grabbed her leg and tucked her so that she fell flat on the bed once more. Micah loomed over her bending low so that his mouth brushed hers.

"Now that we have decided that matter, let's get to the situation at hand," he stated.

She grinned. "And what would that be?"

"You have two very horny mates that need your immediate attention," Micah stated and took her mouth with his, twining and stroking her tongue with his. A tug of her legs spreading them and she felt Merced settle between them. At last the moment she'd been waiting for. It was time to make love with both of her mates.

Chapter Ten

Micah moved from her mouth to nibble along the curve of her face and down the column of her neck. One hand massaged her breast, cupping and shaping before moving to the tip and pinching and tugging at her nipples. The tug seemed to reach right down into her womb and had her pussy clenching with need.

And Merced was right there to take care of that. One hand held her lips spread wide while the other rimmed her opening. His tongue ran through the folds of her sex, up, around and over her clit, torturing her at every pass. She wanted the thrust of his finger deep inside, the suction of his mouth on her clit.

But neither of them gave her what she wanted just yet. Micah moved along her neck and collarbone blazing a trail that felt as if he left fire along her skin. And Merced just kept licking and rimming. She moaned and groaned beneath them arching into their caresses urging them to do more. Her body was a live flame and she needed them to put it out.

Micah chuckled against her skin and his breath fanned over her nipple making it harder and tighter and tearing another cry from her lips. He leant in and ran his tongue around and around the nipple. Her flesh was so tight, it would be impossible for her nipple to get harder. Then he blew across the wet surface and it did. It tightened to the point that her flesh ached.

"Micah," she cried out his name with need but he just smiled at her.

Then Merced shifted his finger and one filled her passage. She lifted her hips taking it as deep as she could and panted for breath. His tongue moved to her clit and flicked over it, back and forth several times before pressing it and rubbing. Just when she felt she might explode he pulled back and just slowly worked his finger in and out.

Micah bent and sucked a nipple into his mouth. Fire streamed and burnt a path through her veins. She arched and screamed. Merced removed his finger and replaced it with his tongue, fucking inside her with it. Her entire body tightened to the point of pain and then with a wild cry she broke. Pleasure coursed through her body and her men kept her right there riding her orgasm for a long wonderful moment.

When they finally let up she collapsed down into the bed. Her body felt boneless and she knew she had a silly smile on her face. Lips met hers and she could taste herself on them. Merced. His tongue rubbed along her bottom lip before his teeth nipped and she opened to him. It was soft and slow and sweet. He pulled slowly from her and her eyes blinked open.

"Do you think you can handle the both of us at once?" he asked softly and just that quick she was on fire again.

She moaned, her whispered "yes," lost as she met his mouth again. Hard and clashing this time. Their tongues stroked and thrust and as he pulled away she scraped his bottom lip with her teeth. Merced grinned and moved to rise from the bed.

"Where are you going?" she demanded.

He laughed. "There is an oil that can be used to coat my flesh so that it is easier for you to accept me," he replied. She watched as he pulled a vial from the pouch Micah usually wore and opened it to pour some into his palm. Holding her gaze he moved his slick palm down to stroke up and down his shaft even running his palm over the head.

She groaned with him and licked her lips. He was slick and she wanted to feel him now. She watched as he moved back across to the bed. Micah moved beside her and she turned to find him on his back one hand wrapped around his cock, the long fingers stroking from base to tip. Leaning low she licked the drop of fluid from the tip and he moaned. Before she could do more than that he used a hand under her chin to urge her to look up at him.

"Rise up and cover me," he urged. "Straddle my hips and take me inside you."

He only had to offer once. She moved to her knees and straddled his hips. Micah gripped her hips and scooted them both so that they were more centred on the bed. She reached down and took his cock in her hand, holding it up while he helped her move to just the right spot. Slowly they lowered her onto him. She felt the nudge of his cock head and moaned as it spread her passage and slowly pushed inside.

Finally she sat on his hips, his cock buried as far as it would go. His hands still held her hips and if not for that she would already be riding up and down on his length.

"Micah," she cried and used her inner muscles to give him a squeeze which had him arching up and surging deeper within.

"Hurry," he breathed out and she felt the dip in the bed. Glancing back she saw Merced joining them, his cock slick and wet with the oil that still gleamed on his palm.

Both of them at once. She could feel her excitement surge as well as her anxiety. Would they fit? They were both big men and she felt small and fragile between them.

"It will feel better than anything that has come before," Merced stated and leaned in to kiss her. With a final nip he turned her back to Micah.

Micah moved his hands up to her shoulders and urged her down to him so that her breasts brushed his chest and their mouths were close. He nipped and licked at her lips slipping his tongue in and out as she moaned. Merced's hands found her hips and caressed them before moving back to her ass. She felt him move so that his knees were between Micah's legs just behind her. She took a deep breath as he began to use the oiled hand to finger her anus.

She was so ready for this, for both of them at once. She moved her mouth from Micah's kiss and let her lips nip and suck at the skin on his neck. Merced shifted and she felt the first press of his cock. Micah had already taken her there earlier and though she was sensitive she really wasn't sore. In fact she had thoroughly enjoyed having him in her ass. She wiggled a little on Micah unable to hold still as the moment she'd been longing for arrived.

Micah groaned and Merced shifted one hand to the small of her back to steady her as he pressed firmly against her. She was already filled with Micah in her pussy and the pressure as Merced eased inside her was almost overwhelming. She groaned and rested her head on Micah's shoulder.

"Just a little more," Merced stated and she could feel the tension in his body as he tried to keep his thrust slow and easy.

The more he entered the greater the pressure. When he was almost in she couldn't hold her groan in. She shook her head against Micah's shoulder giving voice to a keening cry. So good and yet so different. She felt as if her flesh was stretched to the point of tearing. Surely it couldn't take much more. Then with a harsh moan Merced was filling her and she could feel the brush of his sac at her bottom cheeks.

She cried out and bit down on Micah's muscle letting her teeth sink in as she tried to adjust to the overwhelming feeling. So tight. So full. Something had to happen soon or she would split in two.

"Please," she moaned.

Slowly Merced pulled back so that only the head of his cock remained inside her. Her hips were adjusted and then Merced pressed back into her and Micah eased back. With their hands they worked her back and forth on their cocks, one inside and then the other. The pressure lessened and the pleasure increased. Pain existed, a slow burning tug on sensitive tissue and nerve endings not used to such stimulation. But it only seemed to increase the pleasure, the burn and tug an erotic touch she enjoyed.

"More," she breathed, allowing them total control of her body. They moved her and moved within her giving and taking pleasure. The experience was heightened for her and she was sure for them as well, as she could feel the pleasure that her men were receiving. Her senses were on overload. She reeled and spiralled in a place that existed only within the pleasure zone of her body.

Merced moved faster and Micah countered with an equal rhythm that had her panting and moaning. Micah leaned up and took a nipple between his teeth. Merced leaned low and clamped his teeth on the muscle that connected her neck to her shoulder. And she bucked and screamed. Orgasm rushed into her and as she tightened on both of their cocks she could feel the rush of their orgasms as well.

Micah was the first to join her. With a harsh grunt he fucked her, no longer capable of focusing on matching his thrusts to Merced. He just took her and when he came inside her his hips lifted from the bed sending her into Merced and pressing his cock even deeper.

Merced was in the same turmoil, no longer focused on rhythm and all about his release now that he knew she had hers. She knew beyond a doubt that she would always come first with them, no matter the circumstance and it made her feel treasured and loved. As Micah held deep Merced continued thrusting and it was incredible. So good that she felt another orgasm approaching.

Merced pumped hard and fast, his cock giving a constant tug and pull as he rode her ass. As Micah softened a little with release the pressure adjusted and she didn't feel such a savage need. In fact she softened and lay quietly on Micah's chest feeling his breathing slowing as Merced's picked up.

A few more powerful strokes and Merced cried out holding her hips tight and continuing to give small thrusts as his semen filled her. She felt the trigger of another orgasm in her womb and moaned as she trembled with the release. Merced collapsed over her and together the three of them turned so that they were able to lay side by side on the bed. Micah in front of her and Merced behind. She felt sheltered, protected and loved.

Would it always be like this? She believed so. She loved them and knew without a doubt that they felt the same for her. It was a gift of the Danuja that she was happy to experience. She was sure that there would be more and truthfully she was looking forward to it. Anything would be worth the gift that she had been given in these two men, her mates for life.

As she felt them relax into sleep on either side of her she knew that their journey was far from over. This was only the beginning for them all. Wilhelm had to be stopped and she could only pray that the cost would not be too extreme for them to handle. Her mother would be here soon and she couldn't wait for Lydia to meet her mates. At the same time she feared for how her mother would be treated by those who thought her a kidnapper and traitor to the late queen. And she feared what Wilhelm might try to do to Lydia.

They were strong alone and more than formidable together. Merced's powers were still dampened by a spell Wilhelm had used but Micah's no longer were. He would not have the control that Merced did but she was sure they would work together on it. Her sister, the new queen, was back and in charge of the army of warriors. The reigning king was on their side once more and they would have the power of the shifter race beside them as well.

Life was full of surprises, good and bad. Lynx closed her eyes and savoured this moment lying within the arms of her lovers, the flush of pleasure still on them. As long as they were together she could handle all that may lie on the road ahead. For today that would have to be enough. Tomorrow would arrive soon enough.

Epilogue

Wilhelm glared at the man who knelt before him. "What do you mean, her mother lives?"

"The shifter girl," the man stated. "The one who travelled here with the new queen. Her mother is the one who took the girl and raised her with her daughter as if they were sisters."

"Lydia was pregnant," Wilhelm whispered speaking to no one but himself. It was not possible. That could only mean one thing. Slowly a smile spread on his face.

"Sisters?" he asked and laughed as his man nodded.

"Go to the village and find the mother, Lydia is her name," Wilhelm said. "She must never reach them."

The man nodded and made to rise. Wilhelm stopped him with a sword tip to his throat. "Do it yourself this time."

"Yes, sir," was the quick reply. No fear was in the man's eyes and that was why Wilhelm liked him, why he trusted him most. Somehow others always got in the way and screwed them up. Capturing his lovely Lydia was something that was too important now. She had hidden things from him and she would pay for that. He would trust no one else with the task of retrieving her.

"Be quick," Wilhelm said tossing the sword away to clang on the stone floor and shaking his head. "We must have her before the warriors arrive to alert them of things."

"As you wish," his man said and with a bow and nod of his head he was gone.

Wilhelm turned with a smile. Lydia had a daughter and it was the shifter in the castle. He would have to watch the girl a little closer. Regardless they must all die now. But he had some news of his own to share before that happened. And he would enjoy that little task tremendously.

Lydia blinked her eyes as the binding was removed from her eyes.

"This way my lady," she was directed but she noticed he did not remove the magical binding from her neck, the one that denied her ability to shift.

"Plan to tell me where I am now?" she queried and once again was met with a smile and shake of the head.

"All will be explained to you in just a moment, my lady," he said. Always polite. Apologetic even. He could not work for Wilhelm. Lydia had been waiting for years for him to follow her, to find her and kill her.

The door before her opened up and she saw two women at the front of the room in a heated argument. At the sound of the door they both turned and Lydia felt her breath catch in her throat. It couldn't be.

"Serena?" she whispered, not believing her eyes. It couldn't be.

"It has been a long time, my friend," was the reply and there could be no doubt that Serena stood before her.

Lydia had not seen her friend since Serena had been given the task of hiding the queen's sword where Wilhelm could not find it. The Priestess had taken it and Lydia had not seen her again.

She flew across the room and embraced her friend, a sister of her heart and for the first time in a long time she wept.

About the Author

Lacey Thorn spends her days in small town Indiana the proud mother of three. When she is not busy with one of them she can be found typing away on her computer keyboard or burying her nose in a good book. Like every woman she knows just how chaotic life can be and how appealing that great escape can look.

So toss aside the stress and tension of the never ending to do list. For now sit back, relax, and enjoy the ride with Lacey. It's your world…unlaced.

Lacey Thorn loves to hear from readers. You can find her contact information, website details and author profile page at http://www.total-e-bound.com.

11976017R10131

Made in the USA
Charleston, SC
02 April 2012